DEAD BY DESIGN

A MADDIE SWALLOWS MYSTERY

BOOK 5

KAT BELLEMORE

KB PRESS

CHOOSE YOUR OWN ADVENTURE: MYSTERY OR ROMANCE

MADDIE SWALLOWS MYSTERIES

Dead Before Dinner

Dead Upon Arrival

Dead Before I Do

Dead Among Stars

Dead by Design

Dead in the Dark

BORROWING AMOR: New Mexican Romance

Borrowing Amor

Borrowing Love

Borrowing a Fiancé

Borrowing a Billionaire

Borrowing Kisses

Borrowing Second Chances

STARLIGHT RIDGE: Beach Romance

Diving into Love

Resisting Love

Starlight Love

Building on Love

Winning his Love

Returning to Love

Fearless Love

1

The town council meeting hadn't even officially started, and I could already hear the arguing from halfway down Main Street. That wasn't good.

"Maybe we should sit this one out," I whispered to Benji.

He squeezed my hand. "All the more reason for us to attend. They need a voice of reason. It's not like town council can do anything about the purchased land, and riling everyone up will only make things worse."

The residents of Amor had originally been excited when space tourism had set up shop just an hour away, but we hadn't anticipated the repercussions. The celebrities. The pressure for our town to change—to make it more upscale and to the liking of those who stayed overnight before embarking on their two-hour journey to space.

That was also when the real estate developers had set

their sights on our New Mexican town. They'd been stalking us, watching for the weak link that would allow them to sneak in and collect the biggest payday of their careers.

Unfortunately, one of the developers had found that weak link. A vacant piece of land that had been put up for sale when the owner passed away the previous month. It hadn't taken more than a day for Don Mendes to snatch it up. We hadn't even realized it had been on the market until it was too late.

Benji was right. We needed to be in that room. Who knew what crazy thing the town council would propose next. Last I heard, they were talking about making it illegal to sell property to anyone who wasn't an official resident of Amor. And of course, residency was to be determined by town council. Even though I'd grown up here, I had moved away for college. When I'd returned two decades later as a single mom, it had taken months to regain my residency. Town council had questioned my sincerity. Said that I had left once, so what was to stop me from leaving again?

Never mind that I was opening a therapy office in town and had signed a five-year lease. They said it didn't count because my mother was my landlord.

Speaking of my mother.

It was her silver hair I spotted first, piled haphazardly on top of her head. She was standing just outside the entrance to the community center, her gaze scanning the street, as if she were looking for someone.

"Hide me," I told Benji, releasing his hand and moving behind him, forcing him to stop mid-step. "Better yet, you go to the meeting and tell me all about it after."

Benji glanced over his shoulder at me, his eyes crinkled in amusement. "What are you doing?"

"Don't look at me," I whispered, poking him. "She'll see me."

He laughed. "Who, your mom? I thought you two were getting along better these days."

"We are, but I borrowed her waffle maker and may have forgotten the last batch that was cooking. Burned it so badly that the waffle fused with the metal." I paused and peeked around Benji to see if my mom was still there. She was. "She called earlier asking for it back—said she was going to be cooking breakfast tomorrow for the older single ladies' group she's put together."

Benji turned around, ignoring my protests with a patient smile. "I can help you clean it."

And this was why I had fallen in love with my childhood best friend. Because, despite my inheriting a bit of my mother's insanity gene, he was always there by my side. Always my biggest supporter.

As the town's handyman, he was used to fixing things, and it turned out he was skilled at repairing more than just damaged floorboards. My life being one of them. Except, this was one thing I doubted even his incredible skills would be able to take care of.

"I already tried." I tossed a nervous glance over Benji's

shoulder. Shoot. My mom spotted me. Her eyes lit up, and she moved toward where Benji and I stood. "I threw it into a sink of soapy water to soak."

Benji groaned. "You didn't."

By the look on his face, he knew I had.

"I didn't consider what the electronic components might think of the water until it was too late. When I took it to Buck's shop to see if it was fixable, he just laughed." I stopped talking when my mom crossed the street, and I plastered on a smile just as she reached us. "Hey, you snuck up on us. Didn't realize you'd already arrived."

"Been here nearly half an hour already. But I think you already knew that. I saw you hiding behind Benji." My mom placed her hand on my arm and turned me toward the community center. "If you're having second thoughts about coming to this meeting, you should know that I've already put both of your names down to speak."

I stopped mid-step and released an exasperated sigh. She always pulled this kind of stuff on me. "Why would you do that, Mom? We wanted to gauge the room before committing to something like speaking in front of everyone. The council has been very intense lately."

Well, *I* had wanted to gauge the room. Not Benji, though. He always liked to get involved and had intended to address the town whether I chose to or not. It wasn't lost on me that he looked a little too happy about my mom's interference.

She waved a hand through the air, as if I were being

overly dramatic. "That's the council's job, dear. Intensity is the only way to make change happen. Ruby is on the council and, being the mayor's sister, she keeps them from going too far over the line. And it's not like they could actually pass a law to prohibit those outside Amor from purchasing property. It would be unconstitutional."

It wasn't that that worried me. It was the new councilman, Carlos Herrera. I'd always thought him a quiet and thoughtful man until he was elected to the council. Apparently, he'd merely been biding his time, because he'd been passionate, vocal, and downright dangerous ever since. I was concerned that by the end of this meeting, we'd have a riot on our hands.

I gave my mom a weak smile. "If you say so." There was no use arguing with her.

As Benji took my hand and led me across the street, my mom lifted a finger and hurried forward like she had more on her mind. "That reminds me. Did you remember to bring the waffle maker with you?" She looked me over, as if she'd find evidence of it tucked away somewhere.

I was saved from answering when two toddlers dashed in front of me and I had to jump to the side to avoid a collision.

"Sorry, they slipped out of their harnesses," Jake Pletcher called, coming up from behind. He ran after them, holding what looked like two leashes in his hand. On the opposite side of the street, his wife, Angel, had materialized directly in the toddlers' path. In an expert maneuver, she scooped them both up in one fluid motion, and Jake wrangled them into their harnesses and fastened the clips, ensuring they were tight this time.

He removed his bright pink hat and wiped his sleeve across his forehead, breathing hard, and threw an amused look our way. "Interested in adopting twins? Buy one, get one free."

Angel set the twins down on the ground and swatted his arm, though her amused smile suggested she'd be open to the idea. "I'm sure Benji and Maddie have other things on their plate. Can you imagine planning a wedding with these two running around? It would be a disaster."

Jake laughed and replaced his hat before slinging an arm around his wife's shoulders and hanging on to the twins' leashes with his free hand. "Very true."

Wedding?

Benji and I hadn't yet talked about marriage, mostly because I avoided the subject with incredible skill. It had crossed my mind, of course. But we'd only been dating a year. It was too soon to get serious about a life-altering decision like that.

My mom, on the other hand—"The sooner those two marry, the better. Maddie already has two children of her own, you know." She spoke to Jake and Angel with the tone of a wise old sage. "I suppose they aren't children anymore. Lilly's graduated from high school, and Flash will be there soon enough. Regardless, not having a father figure has been difficult for them." She paused and gave a dramatic sigh. "Thank goodness Maddie moved here when she did."

I squeezed my hands into fists to help me hold back the giant eye roll that was lying in wait. I'd only been divorced four years, and yes it had been hard on the kids at first, but it wasn't like they were lacking in love or parental guidance. My mom made it sound like without her, my kids would be dealing drugs on the streets or shoplifting at the local convenience store.

"It's always a delight to see your family," I told the Pletchers, changing the subject. "Are you coming to the town meeting?" I nodded to the community center. The arguing from inside hadn't diminished. If anything, it had gotten louder.

Angel immediately shook her head. "I'm not sure which is worse, those meetings or taking my children to them. I think an early bedtime is the best strategy at this point."

A woman after my own heart.

Jake and Angel gave a little wave as they tried to herd their children along the sidewalk and away from the commotion.

"Maybe we should do what they're doing," I said, attempting to follow them. "An early bedtime sounds wonderful."

My mom grabbed my arm and steered me back toward the front door. "Oh no, you don't. You are a resident of this town, and your voice matters." When I glanced toward

Benji, he lifted a shoulder, as if asking what I expected him to do about it. Probably because he agreed with my mother. That would normally be a strike against someone I was dating.

Good thing I loved him so much.

Unfortunately, this town meeting had nothing to do with love.

The moment we entered that community center, chaos accosted us from every direction, and anxiety filled my chest. I took a step back. "Maybe we should attend the next meeting."

From all appearances, the riot I had feared was already in progress. My elderly neighbor, Edna, was yelling across the room at my friend Debbie, telling her she was going to move from Amor if Debbie dared sell her hair salon to a developer. Debbie was wrapping a strand of her platinum blonde hair around one finger, looking like she was about to cry, insisting she had no such intention.

Cal, our local bicycle shop owner, seemed intimidating at first glance to those who didn't know him, his bald head and tattooed arms on full display this evening. But even he looked like he hadn't escaped the town's wrath. He had managed to get himself trapped at the front of the room and was trying to get out of a conversation with Carlos Herrera, who was animatedly talking, his hands flying through the air.

Bob, a man who was as strict and straitlaced as they came, which was what made him perfect for his position as HR manager at Town Hall, was standing at the front of the room, hammering a gavel he'd purchased for himself, trying to get everyone to calm down.

"We won't accomplish anything like this," he shouted, trying to be heard above the crowd.

No one listened.

Benji brought two fingers to his lips and released an ear-splitting whistle. It had the desired effect, all conversation coming to an immediate halt, but I wished he would have warned me beforehand. My ears rang for a full five minutes afterwards.

Bob cleared his throat. "Thank you. Now, will my fellow town council members join me up here? We have a lot to discuss this evening, and I'd prefer to be able to hear what each of you has to say, as opposed to," he waved a hand around, "this." His gaze scanned the room as everyone found their seats. "Where is Mayor Freedman?"

"He's running a few minutes late," the mayor's sister Ruby said, taking her seat at the front. "He asked that you start without him."

Carlos Herrera took the seat next to her and snorted. "Yes, I'm sure he did. Afraid to face the music, is he?"

Bob gave Carlos a reproachful look. "You know the mayor is a busy man." He then turned his attention to the rest of the room, clearly nervous as he struggled to formulate his thoughts. "I appreciate everyone coming to our meeting this evening. It's been several months since the real estate developers began descending on our town. Now that there have been three successful flights out at the spaceport, they've become more aggressive."

"At least most of them can accept no as an answer," Debbie said from where she sat next to my mom. "This new guy, Don Mendes, is trouble. He's been making promises he can't keep and hiding all sorts of fine print in his contracts. Thankfully, no one has sold their store to him, or they'd find themselves at the raw end of the deal."

"Did you notice his hair?" Edna added, subconsciously patting her own gray hair at the same time. "That shade of red is something you only find in horror movies—you can tell a lot about someone from their hair." She looked to Debbie to back her up.

Debbie shrugged. "It's true."

Edna gave a satisfied nod and turned back to Bob. "If you ask me, we should have run him out of town the second he arrived."

I was unsure if Edna was more offended by his hair or his presence here in town, but regardless, nearly every head in the room was nodding in agreement.

"Yes, I've heard of his less-than-honest business dealings," Bob said. "And we all agree we don't want the developers to build here. But with the sale of that old piece of land to the likes of Don Mendes, what are we going to do to stop them? Mr. Mendes has just made himself a part of Amor, and he didn't need our help to do it."

"Does anyone know what his company intends to do with the land?" Benji asked from beside me. "He only purchased the land three weeks ago, and construction has already begun. He's not wasting any time."

Bob hesitated. "Nothing is final."

"Nothing's final?" Carlos said, incredulous. "There is an actual wooden frame on the lot, and it looks like it's the beginning of something big. Bob, you see everything that goes on in Town Hall. You hear everything. At least be honest with the people of Amor. They deserve that much. I heard Mr. Mendes is building a nine-story luxury hotel, complete with a five-star rooftop restaurant."

Whispering broke out. If that were true, the building would tower over the rest of Amor, and we wouldn't even be able to afford to stay there if we wanted to. It would taunt us with its inaccessibility. And once this hotel was built, others would follow. High-end restaurants and clothing shops. Old stores would be torn down to make room for the new. The things that made Amor special would disappear. More money would come into our town, sure. That was how the developers were trying to sell it. But we would lose our identity in the process.

Bob looked uncomfortable, opening his mouth to speak but then closing it again. "I don't know where you got your information, Mr. Herrera, but Don Mendes purchased the land legally," he finally said. "His company is free to build anything they like, as long as it falls within the legal limits of commercial construction."

"But we can stop him from obtaining any further permits and licenses," Carlos said. "We can make it so difficult that he gives up and leaves. Once other developers hear how inhospitable a place Amor is, they'll stop trying as well."

My mom shot to her feet, and I shrank into my seat. I had been on the receiving end of my mom's disapproval countless times, and from her pinched expression, Carlos was about to get a taste of what she was capable of.

"Is that what you want the world to know us as? Inhospitable?" she asked. "Because you're right. Word will get around. And no one will want to come here. They will drive past us, just so they don't have to be subjected to our inhospitality."

Carlos didn't back down. Instead, my mom's words seemed to fuel his fire. "Good. We have enough people as is. If you ask me, we're better off without them."

My mom's hands balled into fists, and her eyes narrowed. "That's the thing. No one did ask you, and yet you go around town spreading your opinions and ill-advised ideas to anyone who has the misfortune of being in your way." She then turned so she was addressing the room. "If we shun everyone who isn't originally from here, it won't take long before we become just another ghost town. And no one will remember us."

"You saying that you like the idea of all these developers swooping in and taking over?" Carlos asked, his brows dipping in anger and frustration.

Bob hammered his gavel and tried to get things back on track, but my mom talked over him.

"Of course not. But there are better ways to go about it. Aggression isn't the answer."

"Aggression is the only language these people understand," Carlos shot back.

The back door to the community center opened with a prolonged creak, and every head turned to see who the latecomer was.

Sheriff Potts and Mayor Freedman stood in the open doorway.

"Unfortunately, that's the kind of attitude that could get you in loads of trouble," the sheriff said, folding her arms across her chest. "Especially because Don Mendes has gone missing. And I suspect that someone in this room had something to do with it."

2

I'd never seen a town council meeting empty out so fast. If Sheriff Danielle Potts thought she was going to question people, she should have sealed the door first. My mom was the first to disappear, with members of town council close behind. Less than two minutes after the sheriff's pronouncement, only she, Mayor Freedman, Benji, and I were left.

"Was it something I said?" she asked with a wry smile.

It was nice that she found something humorous about this situation. "Danielle, you just accused half the town of either kidnapping or killing the one person that everyone has a unified hatred of."

She gave a small nod. "Yes, I did."

I released a heavy breath. "It was bad enough that an international celebrity was murdered at the spaceport just a few months back. The fact that people are still willing to come out here is nothing short of a miracle. But if we develop a trend of visitors disappearing and being murdered, we're going to have a real problem on our hands. We need the business the spaceport brings. The employment. The wealthy guests."

Mayor Freedman eyed me. "So, you aren't against the recent attempts at development?"

"No," I said, though I avoided Benji's gaze. Those who had lived in Amor their entire lives were the ones who would fight these real estate developers with their dying breath, my boyfriend included. "We need to grow if we're going to survive."

"Whether or not these developers have a place here in Amor isn't the real issue," Benji said, turning his gaze on the sheriff. "Do you really think one of us did something to Don Mendes? He's only one individual representing a large corporation. Him disappearing won't stop construction."

"No, but it might cause them to think twice about further development," the mayor mused.

Danielle nodded in agreement. "I hate to think folks in this town are capable of something like that, but who else has the motive?"

"Other developers," I said. "There are a couple of them in town at the moment, aren't there?"

Mayor Freedman hesitated. "One. But he was only here for a couple of days. He left this morning. Hardly enough time to make enemies."

"But plenty of time to kill someone," Danielle said.

From the look the mayor sent the sheriff, it was clear that there was more to this lone developer than he was letting on. A personal connection of some kind, and the mayor didn't want us going anywhere near him. Benji caught it too.

"Sam," he said, "how closely do you work with these real estate developers?"

"Only as close as necessary." Mayor Freedman glanced at his phone, then Danielle. "You have a missing person to find, so I'll leave you to it."

Everything about this was odd to me. The sheriff and mayor showing up, announcing the disappearance of Don Mendes the way they had. No details. The only thing Danielle had managed to do was instill panic. I doubted that had been her objective.

Then again, maybe it had.

"How do you know Don Mendes didn't just leave town?" I asked Danielle as Sam hurried out.

"The hotel called a couple of hours ago," she said. "Don had a Do Not Disturb sign on his door for the past two days. They finally went in this afternoon, concerned. The place was trashed—drawers emptied, clothes thrown around. And no sign of Don."

Benji spoke up, his forehead scrunched like he was in deep thought. "When you burst in here tonight, you were looking for reactions. Someone who wasn't as surprised as they should have been—someone who looked guilty, maybe."

Danielle barked out a single laugh. "I was looking for someone who seemed panicked and felt the need to slip out early to avoid questioning. And then the entire room cleared out. Obviously not my best idea." And then the sheriff gave me a familiar look—one that told me she was getting a little too comfortable with asking for advice. When she'd first moved to town, she'd refused any help I offered. But she'd loosened up since then and now seemed to have no qualms with asking for my assistance.

I knew how important finding this guy was, but what the sheriff refused to believe was that I never intentionally placed myself in her investigations, and I was finally in a situation where I had some stability in my life.

My and my roommate's therapy office was thriving, my kids, Lilly and Flash, had finally forgiven me for moving them to my former hometown after their father and I had divorced, and I was in the best relationship of my life with Benji. Even my mother and I were beginning to get along —as well as could be expected, anyway.

I wasn't going to mess that all up by involving myself with a missing real estate developer. That was the sheriff's job. And if she had a problem with that, she could schedule a therapy appointment and tell me all about it.

"Well, you tried. Can't ask for more than that," I said, moving past her to leave.

Benji followed with a quick goodbye, and we stepped

out into the crisp evening air. "I'm proud of you, not getting sucked into another one of the sheriff's investigations," he told me, taking my hand. "Though I have to admit, it's coming from a selfish place. That mess at the spaceport a few months back—I couldn't sleep until you arrived home safe, and I never want to have to go through that again."

"I wasn't going to ask for your help," Danielle called from the doorway. She'd apparently followed us out. "I'm good at my job and can read people just as well as you, Maddie."

I gave her a small wave over my shoulder. "I know."

But even as we walked away, my mind was already spinning. Why kidnap Don in the first place? If someone really did want him out of the way—permanently—why had his room been ransacked? They had to have been looking for something. All the official licenses, blueprints, and anything related to his job would be electronic and on file with his company, so that wouldn't be it.

"You're doing it again," Benji said, his lips tugging up at the corners.

"What?" I asked, forcing my thoughts to return to the here and now. The starlit night. The man holding my hand —the same man I'd grown up with and had never dared dream I'd love with the intensity I did. And that he'd return those feelings.

"You're thinking about the sheriff's case. The one you

told her she could handle on her own—and that you had no intention of getting involved with."

"Am not." I gave him my widest grin to prove it, but as we passed Cal's bike shop, the lights flickered on and then just as quickly turned off. My smile faltered. "Do you think Cal returned to the shop after the meeting cleared out?"

Benji was still walking with his long stride, not having seemed to notice anything out of the ordinary. "Maybe, though I doubt it. Cal is a man who appreciates his time away from his store."

I slowed my steps, but Benji's momentum carried me forward. "Someone is inside."

More to humor me than anything else, Benji backed up and peered through the windows. "Everything looks okay to me." And then he grabbed the front door handle and pulled to prove it. The door didn't budge—it was locked.

"Must have been my eyes playing tricks on me," I said, though I didn't believe it. But it was better for Benji to think I had poor eyesight than question my sanity.

By the time we reached my house, however, I would have preferred he assume his girlfriend was losing her mind. That would have been better than finding a man I'd never seen before stooped amongst my bushes and peering through the windows just as Benji had done at the bike shop ten minutes earlier. And better he think I'm crazy than the front door fly open, my son, Flash, tearing through the doorway, baseball bat raised, as if he knew what to do with a piece of sports equipment.

Lilly came running out after her brother with my roommate Trish close behind her, all yelling like lunatics. Trish's cat Ava zoomed out after them but had no idea what was going on, instead running around and whacking everyone with her paw before ultimately spinning around and running back inside.

That was a good call, and I thought we should all follow the cat's example, but then the man screamed and dropped to the ground, hands raised above his shaved head. Whoever he was, he looked to be no threat to my terrifying family.

"What in the world is going on here?" Benji asked, running up the walkway.

"Please don't hurt me," the man whimpered. He slowly reached a hand into his shirt pocket, and Flash shook the baseball bat at him in what was supposed to be a menacing act of dominance. In reality, it looked more like he was swatting at mosquitos, but it was enough to make the man whimper again. "I have a card."

"This guy pounded on the door like he wanted to murder everyone inside," Flash told Benji.

And so, of course, the first thing my teenage son had done was run outside after him. It was a miracle my kids had survived as long as they had.

"I was about to call Sheriff Potts when the kids took off," Trish said, her breaths heavy.

I strode up to the man, who was still cowering on the ground, his raised hand now holding the card he'd risked his life to procure. After a brief hesitation, I pulled it from his fingers.

It was too dark outside to read it, so I pulled my phone out and turned on the flashlight. It only took a quick glance to know whose business card this was.

It was mine.

"First question. Who are you?"

The man sucked in a shuddered breath. "My name is Don Mendes."

3

Don Mendes was at my house. A man who was supposedly missing. Possibly kidnapped. More likely dead.

"Don Mendes?" I repeated, making sure I hadn't misheard.

He gave a little nod. "I work for a company that owns land on the other side of town."

My gaze found Benji. He looked just as shocked as I felt. "Why do you have my business card?" I asked, turning my attention back to Don.

Don hesitated. "I think someone is trying to kill me."

After the insanity of that evening's town council meeting, the idea wasn't completely farfetched. "So, why don't you go to the police? Sheriff Potts can help you. As it turns out, she believes you are a missing person and has been searching the entire town for you. If you stopped by her office, you'd be doing both of you a favor."

Don harrumphed. "She can keep looking, for all I care. I did visit your sheriff two days ago. But she wouldn't believe me. Said that faulty electrical outlets was part of staying in an old hotel. As if flickering lights and TVs turning off and on was normal. When I asked about the pastry I'd bought that made me ill for three days or the man who tried to run me over with his bicycle, she said I was making too big a deal out of normal life events."

Benji gave a small nod. "I remember fixing the outlets in your room. Buck, our electrical guy, wasn't available at the time, and the hotel asked me to make it a priority."

"I think he's telling the truth," Flash said, startling me. In my shock, I'd forgotten he and his sister were still out here.

"Thank you for your input," I told him. "But it's time you and Lilly head back inside. You have school in the morning."

"I don't," Lilly said. "And I'm legally an adult now, which means I can make my own decisions."

Both valid points, but I still didn't want her or her brother anywhere near this guy.

I gave her my best mom look. "And you still live in my house. Inside. Now."

Both Flash and Lilly opened their mouths to protest, but Trish ushered them inside before they had the chance. I mouthed *thank you,* and she gave me a tight smile in return. Not only had this man terrified her and the kids tonight, but he knew where we lived. Even if I managed to get rid of him for the evening, there was nothing stopping him from coming back.

"Faulty outlets, sketchy pastry, and a man on a bicycle who nearly collided with you," I listed. "I've experienced all of that."

Don's lips pulled into a frown. "I understand they seem like mundane things. But when they all happen to the same person on the same day, it doesn't make sense. No one has luck that bad. The guy on the bike nearly ran me over on two separate occasions, both within a couple of hours of each other."

He had a point. That was an awful lot in such a short period of time.

"Okay, let's say you're right and someone is trying to kill you. Why are you here? This isn't exactly my area of expertise."

Don straightened, his eyes flashing in my direction. "The sheriff must have thought I had lost my mind because she gave me your card. Said you might be able to help. Do I look like a crazy man to you?"

In that moment? Yes, quite. The sudden intensity behind his eyes was alarming. Don no longer looked like someone to be pitied but rather someone I feared. I'd heard of his antics to get local businesses to sell to him, and I'd thought the owners had exaggerated to get town council on their side. I no longer doubted them.

I took a step toward Benji. My home address wasn't on the business card, which meant he'd asked around and tracked me down. Not too difficult, but it was still a bit unnerving.

"Why don't you stop by my office tomorrow morning? I'll fit you in first thing at eight-thirty, and we can talk more about it then."

Don was already shaking his head before I'd finished speaking. "They'll come back tonight. And this time, I don't think I'll be so lucky."

"They?" Benji asked. His expression was thoughtful. Almost like he believed Don. But that would make Benji as crazy as Don likely was.

Don latched on, a glimmer of hope passing over his features. It quickly morphed into dread. "The shadows that follow me. The ones that make things happen during the day and haunt me at night. They dump out my drawers and rattle the suitcases. I think they're trying to tell me to leave town—telling me I'm not wanted here. If I don't listen, it's only going to get worse."

Benji released a long sigh. "I see." He rubbed an eyebrow. "I believe you, Don. And I'll see to it that the shadows don't bother you tonight."

I tried to catch his eye, warn him that he should be careful making promises he couldn't keep. Telling the man he wouldn't dream of demons wasn't going to make it so. Though the ransacked hotel room hadn't been in his head. That had been very real.

Benji refused to meet my gaze.

And then Don did something so unexpected, it left me speechless and staring.

He wrapped Benji in a hug.

"Thank you," he repeated over and over. "Thank you. Thank you."

I didn't know what Benji had noticed that I hadn't, but I sincerely hoped it didn't backfire in Don's therapy session the next morning. Because if those demons showed up tonight, I was going to be the one who took the blame.

THE NEXT MORNING, I pushed snooze three times before I managed to roll out of bed. I hadn't slept at all, imagining Don showing up and pounding on our door in the middle of the night because the shadows had returned. The pounding hadn't appeared, though, and I was left with a fuzzy brain and the inability to focus as I dragged myself into the office.

I glanced at my phone. No new texts. I had expected at least a thank you from the sheriff after I'd let her know that Don had been found and was on his way back to his hotel room. It wasn't until then that I realized I'd written the text but had forgotten to push send.

Well, better late than never.

The sooner this Don Mendes situation was taken care of, the better, because he was seriously messing with my psyche. Thankfully Trish hadn't had the same problem.

She'd left the house a full thirty minutes earlier than me to open the office. Every day I thanked my lucky stars she'd decided to leave the big city and follow me here to this remote New Mexican town. I didn't know what I'd do without her.

"You okay?" Clarisse, our receptionist, asked me as I trudged in. Her brows dipped in concern. "You look awful."

"Didn't sleep." It was probably obvious as I fumbled with the key to my office door. It took five tries to get it open. "I have an eight-thirty appointment that isn't in the books. Just send him in when he gets here—no need to fill out insurance forms. This one will be on the house."

Clarisse raised a curious eyebrow but knew better than to ask questions, especially considering my current state. "You got it, boss."

I tossed my purse under the desk and slipped into my chair, leaning back with a heavy head. What I needed was a good dose of coffee. Or tea. Any caffeinated beverage would do. In fact, the more, the better.

Too bad I'd given up caffeine the previous week. Told Clarisse to hide the coffee machine because I was going cold turkey. Apparently, I'd thought it had been a good idea to go healthy—as if I were capable of it. I now cursed last week's Maddie. How dare she deprive me of my sole source of sanity? Coffee was how I got through life nowadays.

Of course, that had been the very reason I'd decided to

give caffeine up in the first place and replace it with the natural highs of life—exercise and fresh fruits and vegetables.

It had been a terrible idea.

"Clarisse," I called. "Coffee. I need all of it. Whatever you got."

She showed up in the doorway, a slight smile pulling on her lips and a mug in hand. "Already waiting for you."

I was torn between being grateful for such an amazing human being and being annoyed that she hadn't done as I'd asked. "I thought I told you that no matter the amount of pleading and begging, you were not to allow me to have anything that wasn't on the approved healthy eating list. And that cup of coffee isn't on there."

Her smile dipped, and she seemed perplexed, as if she was unsure if she was in trouble.

I held out my hands toward the coffee cup and grinned to let her know she'd done well. The grateful part of me had won out. Healthy Maddie would have to wait a day— or two. "Thank you for ignoring me. This coffee is going to save lives."

Clarisse smirked. "Your life or your patients'?"

"Both."

She laughed as she left, and I sipped my coffee. I would have guzzled it if it hadn't been so hot. I needed a clear head for this appointment.

But eight-thirty came and went, and Don Mendes never showed. I didn't have a phone number for him, so instead I called the hotel. He had to have returned to his room the previous evening—he had nowhere else to go.

"I thought you'd have heard about the fiasco at the town meeting last night," the hotel receptionist told me after I requested to be connected to his room. "Mr. Mendes hasn't been seen for nearly three days."

"I see. Were you the one who contacted the sheriff?"

"No," she said. "That was my manager."

"Would you mind connecting me with his room anyway?" I asked. "If he doesn't answer, I'd appreciate if you could physically check the room. Last night didn't exactly go well, and he may be purposely avoiding you."

The receptionist didn't seem excited at the prospect, but after I asked if she'd rather get the sheriff involved, she finally relented and placed me on hold.

I drummed my fingers on my desk as I waited. A quick glance into my coffee mug told me it was empty, and it left me feeling both sad and relieved. Old habits die hard, and I didn't think I was quite ready to let go of this one.

When the hotel receptionist returned, she gave me the news I'd half-expected.

Don Mendes wasn't in his room. She'd discovered something odd, though. Mr. Mendes's suitcase was missing, as were the comforter and pillow from the bed. They had been there the previous day when the sheriff had stopped by to look around the room, and no one had seen Mr. Mendes come or go.

So, Don had been there but hadn't stayed. Where had he gone off to?

"Sorry, one last question. Have you been having trouble with electrical outlets on that floor? Maybe some recent construction in that part of the building?"

A pause on the other end of the line.

"No construction, though Mr. Mendes did complain about the outlets, and we discovered that the ones for his room did have faulty wiring. Benji fixed them the next day."

"And no other rooms have had issues with the wiring? Just that one?" I pressed.

It was a difficult balance as a psychologist. If you didn't press your patient to talk, they might never get the help they needed. But if you pressed too much, you came across as harsh or nosy, and they clammed right up. In this case, I fell into the latter group.

"No, just the one room. And if you have further questions, you can contact Sheriff Potts. She has been apprised of the situation." And then she hung up.

Well, that was a dead end. Maybe Don had decided to leave town, scared off by whoever had been messing with him. But then why take the bedding?

My phone burst to life, and I grabbed at it, hoping it was Don apologizing for the missed appointment.

Benji's face filled the screen, and as much as I loved him, I couldn't help the disappointment that washed over me.

"Hey, hon," I said, attempting to sound upbeat and not at all worried about a man I didn't know and shouldn't care about.

Silence.

"Benji, is everything okay?"

His breaths came fast and heavy. "No, it's not. Do you have a free moment?"

I glanced at the clock on the wall. There was no way Don was showing up for his appointment now. "Yeah, I had a no-show."

"Then you'll want to hurry out to the new construction site on the edge of town."

My brain worked double-time, trying to make sense of what Benji was telling me. "You mean the high-rise that Don Mendes's company is building?"

"Yeah. Except it's not so high anymore. It's been burned to the ground."

4

I didn't ask further questions, just said, "Be right there," grabbed my purse, and bolted out of the office. The land Don's company had purchased was on the opposite side of town, and thankfully I had driven my car to work that day. I didn't always.

When I neared the location, I slowed, not because I was nervous about what I'd find but because I must have been the last one to arrive. At least a hundred people were gathered around the site, both in the street and on the sidewalks. The sheriff's car and the town's fire truck were the only vehicles that had made it through the crowd.

Even with all the people blocking my ability to get closer, I could see what had brought them together.

Just yesterday on this piece of land had stood the beginnings of a hotel that, once it was completed, would have mocked our town with its elegance.

Now?

Most of the structure had crumbled, and what still stood was burned beyond repair. It would all need to come down. I glanced uneasily around the crowd. There was no way this fire was an accident. And these were no longer minor attempts to get Don Mendes to leave town. This was arson. Sabotage. Criminal. And that person could be standing among us here.

I haphazardly parked the car and jumped out. I spotted Benji on the opposite side of the crowd. "Benji," I called, slipping between the gathered onlookers and making my way to him.

He stood on his tiptoes to better see over their heads, his gaze scanning the crowd until it landed on me. When I'd reached him, he pulled me into a hug. "You okay?" he asked.

I gave him a squeeze. "Yeah, I'm all right." I nodded toward the burned building. "When did this happen?"

Benji shrugged. "Sometime during the night, I think. Lou put it out a while ago, but he's just now deemed it safe for the sheriff to do her thing."

Now that I had a better view, I could see Danielle walking carefully around the perimeter, her deputy taking photographs. Lou was walking through the middle of the construction site, his steps slow, as if he were looking for something specific.

"Any idea what started it?" I whispered. It was silly for me to keep my voice down, considering no one else was.

But I wanted to make sure Danielle and Lou were able to concentrate on what they were doing. Serious crime wasn't something we had a problem with in Amor. Other than the double homicide a few years back, of course. But that was a one-off event. Usually, the sheriff was busy with teenage pranksters. Petty theft. Vandalism. That sort of thing.

Not arson.

"I don't think they know yet," Benji whispered back. "But..." He hesitated and glanced around us.

"What?"

He gave a quick shake of his head. "Later."

Benji knew something he didn't want all these people to be privy to, and if any of them overheard, the entire town would know before lunchtime. But his hesitancy only made me more curious, and I didn't think I could wait.

I was about to suggest that he and I get out of there when Lou shouted from across the construction site, "Sheriff, over here."

From the urgency in his voice, Lou had found something that troubled him. He held an object out to Danielle, but I couldn't tell what it was until she opened it.

A wallet.

She shook soot off it and then looked through whatever contents had managed to survive the fire.

A pause, and then her gaze shot up and searched the crowd. It didn't settle until it landed directly on me.

Danielle lifted a finger and pointed it at me, motioning for me to cross the line. I hesitated, having no desire to be a part of what they had discovered. But then she lifted an eyebrow, giving me a look that said *Really?*

I ducked under the police tape, to the protest of those who hadn't seen the sheriff's summons, and tiptoed my way through the wreckage.

"Don's wallet," she said when I reached her. "The leather protected the contents. Mostly." In her hand was what remained of the business card she'd given him when she'd accused him of being crazy. My business card. She held it up for me to see.

I nodded slowly, and Danielle waited, as if expecting me to have some sort of reaction to that bit of news. "So what, his wallet is here," I finally said, having no idea what she was alluding to. "That means he was here at some point, like you'd expect, considering he's the one who procured the land and the permits to build on it."

The sheriff remained quiet, studying me, like there was something I wasn't grasping and she was waiting to see if I'd catch on. It was annoying.

"You don't think Don started the fire, do you?" I said. "What reason would he have to destroy his own construction site?"

"Did he make an appointment with you?" she asked, ignoring my questions. That was why she had called me over. Not because of the wallet but because of the card.

My gaze took in our surroundings. "Yes. He was supposed to see me this morning. He never showed up."

Lou walked over, his expression grim. "It would have been a miracle if he had." He nodded to the right of us, where he'd been lifting boards.

It took me a moment to see what he was referring to, but when I did, I promptly turned away.

There was Don Mendes in the center of the construction site, buried under blackened structural beams. His unseeing eyes accused me of putting him off until morning. He had been in danger. He had been scared. No one had believed him. And now he was dead.

"I guess this is where he disappeared to," Danielle murmured.

I stilled, realizing she hadn't seen my text yet. She didn't know I'd seen Don and that last night, he'd been very much alive.

Lou walked back to Don and moved a few additional boards. He paused, then lifted a piece of cloth that had holes burned in it. "He was sleeping here. This is flame-retardant bedding—like the kind they use in hotels."

"Why was he here instead of his room?" Danielle mused.

I glanced back to where Benji waited outside the police tape, and wondered how much I should tell the sheriff.

"Maddie?" Danielle said. "Everything okay?"

My attention turned back to her, my mind made up. I

couldn't withhold information. Not if it would help catch whoever had done this. "It wasn't an accident."

"We know that," she said. "Lou found multiple points of origin. This was arson." Danielle studied me again for a moment. "Did something happen?"

My gaze took in the burned lumber but avoided the area where Don had been buried by it. I desperately hoped he'd already been dead when the building came crashing down around him. "It's true that he did miss his appointment this morning, but I spoke with him last night."

Danielle took a step toward me. "He called last night, and you didn't tell me?"

"I sent you a text, sort of, but no, he didn't call," I said slowly. "He came by the house, frantic. Said someone was after him." I hesitated. "He said you thought he was losing his mind."

A shadow crossed over the sheriff's face, and her defenses were immediately raised. "He was raving like a lunatic," she said, her words quick. "Telling me that demons were after him and he needed protection. What was I supposed to think?"

I could understand her point of view. Even I had put off his concerns until morning. And at the time he had gone to the sheriff, no crime had been committed. The man's hotel room had issues with electricity. Someone lost control on their bike. The man got food poisoning. Nothing had indicated the need for law enforcement.

"This isn't your fault," I said. "Anyone else would have handled it the same way."

"Of course this isn't my fault," she snapped. "After his initial request, I never saw him again. I figured he'd let himself out of town, tired of the residents complaining and filing baseless charges against him."

"Folks were filing criminal charges against him?" I asked, my interest piqued. This was the first I'd heard of that.

Danielle harrumphed. "Yeah, and I had to waste my time checking each one of them out. None of them stuck, of course. The complaints stopped a few days ago, and I thought people had finally moved on and accepted the situation for what it was." She looked around at the debris. "I guess not."

A few days ago. That was around the same time these other incidents had begun. Almost as if when someone had realized the sheriff wasn't going to do something about Don Mendes, they had decided they'd take things into their own hands.

I needed to talk to Benji.

"Well, that's all I know, so I'll let you get back to your investigation," I said, backing away.

Danielle watched me with a skeptical eye but didn't stop me. "You know more than you're saying. Something else happened last night when he came to your house."

"Nothing else did, I promise," I said. "I made the

appointment with him for this morning so we could talk
further."

Guilt once again washed over me. I should have
helped him.

But what would I have done? I had honestly thought
the man was psychotic. It wasn't like I was going to offer to
harbor him in my home, where my children were.

The sheriff gave a single nod, though she didn't look
like she believed me.

As soon as I'd ducked under the crime scene tape,
Benji appeared at my side.

"What happened in there?" he asked, his voice low.

I glanced around at the bystanders. The crowd hadn't
dissipated. If anything, it had grown.

"Not here," I murmured. "My office. I'll drive you."

Benji placed a hand on the small of my back. "I
brought the truck. How about if I pick up muffins from the
diner and meet you there?"

Even in times of crisis, Benji knew exactly what I
needed.

"Make them double chocolate chip," I said, throwing
him a side glance. "We're going to need it."

5

I paced the Amor Therapy Services waiting room as I waited for Benji. There had been no need to cancel the day's appointments; my patients had taken care of that themselves. As soon as word had spread about the fire, every shop in town had closed, every appointment canceled—everyone wanting a front-row seat. The only thing still open would be the schools, but even then, I was certain it wasn't by choice. How would it look, though, if all the children were let loose while the teachers scurried across town so they could gawk at the remains of Don Mendes and his fancy hotel?

"Why isn't he here yet?" I asked Trish. Clarisse had left the office right after I had—got a call from her brother telling her about all the commotion at the construction site—so Trish had stayed. My roommate and business partner hadn't grown up in Amor and hadn't yet acquired the town's small-town gossip tendencies. If she stayed long enough, she would.

"He'll be here," she said, though her own nervousness was apparent as she combed her fingers though her shoulder-length blue hair.

Footsteps thundered on the stairwell just outside the door, and it burst open.

It wasn't Benji.

My son, Flash, flew into the waiting room with his older sister on his heels.

"Is it true?" he asked without preamble, as if it were perfectly normal for him to not be at school midmorning. As if he normally visited me at work. "Did that new construction site burn to the ground? Everyone is saying Mr. Herrera did it. They claim he threatened these real estate developers would get what was coming to them, and it looks like he made good on his promise."

My children, unlike Trish, had absolutely acquired the town's gossip habits. Or maybe that was just a byproduct of being a teenager. Flash's eyes were eager, and he hopped excitedly from foot to foot.

"Aren't you supposed to be learning calculus right now?" I asked, glancing at the clock on the wall. "Or do they let all the kids out in the streets every time a fire breaks out?"

Lilly answered for her brother, stepping up beside him and looking just as excited. She held her camera in one hand, looking ready to jump into action. "Grandma picked him up after swinging by to collect me from the nature reserve. The roadrunners and cactuses won't mind waiting another day to be photographed."

Grandma. Of course. This excitement the kids had for gossip and jumping into situations where they didn't belong wasn't just a teenager thing...it was genetic.

"Where is she?" I asked, releasing a defeated sigh.

"Right here," she sang, bustling in. She was about to shut the door when she stopped abruptly and spoke to someone outside. After a curt "Not now," she slammed it shut.

"Who was that?" I asked.

My mom waved a hand through the air. "Benji. Said he needed to talk to you, but right now we have family matters to discuss. Just because you two are dating doesn't mean he can nose his way in whenever he feels like it."

"Mom," I said with a groan, and slipped past her, hoping he hadn't driven off yet. He hadn't. Instead, he was leaning against his truck, wearing a smirk.

"I figured you'd be by to rescue me," he said.

That was one way to put it. But I'd hoped that he'd be the one doing the rescuing. "I'm so sorry. I don't know why she has to be like that. Want to go for a drive, and we can talk about what happened at the construction site?"

Benji nodded toward my office. "Think they'll allow that?"

When I turned back, three faces were watching us through the window, not at all embarrassed at being caught. On the contrary, Flash and Lilly waved, and then my mom motioned for us to come in.

"Or we could enter the insanity that is awaiting us and involve my family in something they shouldn't be anywhere near."

Benji laughed. "As frustrating as it is for you, I kind of like that they want to be included. They're your family, and how long are Flash and Lilly going to be around? You'll miss this, you know." He glanced at the window, the three faces still watching, probably making sure we wouldn't jump in the car and make an escape attempt.

"If you're sure," I said, taking his hand and leading him toward the office. "But my mom has to accept that you're part of this family. She does this to Trish all the time—excludes her. And she didn't do that to you until we started dating. She says she's happy for me, but in reality, she feels threatened. She's afraid you're taking me away from her and I'll leave all over again."

"Well, Madame Psychologist, you can assure her that that is never going to happen. I plan on staying in Amor until the day I die."

I stumbled. That was an awfully big statement—and a very long time. I loved Amor and did plan on staying for a while. But until the day I died?

"You okay?" Benji asked, his brows creased in concern.

"Yeah, just clumsy," I said, tossing him a smile. No need to get into matters of longevity. There would be plenty of time to think about that later. Or maybe just avoid the subject entirely. I was good at that.

"I KNEW IT," my mom said. "When Don Mendes went missing, it was only a matter of time."

My family was seated in the therapy office's waiting room, Benji and I leaning against the reception desk. I'd invited Trish to join us, but she'd excused herself. She'd never enjoyed interfering in the sheriff's business like my family had.

I turned my attention back to my mom. "He didn't go missing because he died," I said. "He came by our house last night, terrified. Someone in town has been trying to scare him into leaving."

Benji gave a slow nod. "Yeah, and I know who."

All eyes turned to him, and when he didn't immediately start speaking, Flash and Lilly simultaneously said, "Well?"

He gave an exaggerated shake of his head, pretending to be disappointed. "And I thought you guys were detectives." When it was clear we didn't understand what he was getting at, he pulled out a legal pad of paper. "There are five store owners that Don Mendes was harassing."

"Yeah, their shops all border the park," I said. "I heard a rumor that Don's company wants to build a high-end shopping complex or something like that."

Benji pointed at me. "Right. And who are the store owners?"

"Debbie has her hair salon," I said.

My mom held up her hand as if we were back in school. "Cal Rodriguez owns the bike shop."

Benji was nodding as he wrote. "Keep going."

"The bakery," Lilly added. "Rebecca owns that."

Benji wrote it down. "Two more."

"The electronics repair shop," Flash excitedly said. "Buck fixed my computer a few months ago."

"And finally?" Benji asked, glancing up from the pad of paper.

"The hardware store," I said. "Jake's place."

Benji held up the list of shops for us to see, and my mind began racing through all the incidents that Don had told us had occurred. This must have been what had spooked Benji the previous evening. He'd put it all together.

"But...they aren't the type," I said, not wanting to believe what was right in front of me.

"The type to do what?" my mom asked, sounding annoyed that I knew something she didn't.

I hesitated, unsure if I should voice the obvious conclusion. My mom wasn't exactly known for being able to keep things to herself.

"Well?" my kids said again, also seeming annoyed that they had to keep prompting us to tell what we knew.

"I'd assumed it was one person who was trying to scare

Don away," I said. "But he received food poisoning from the bakery. And the electrical outlets were messed up in his hotel room, and his was the only one."

I raised an eyebrow, prompting my family to catch on.

"Don't forget that someone on a bicycle nearly collided with him," Benji added. "Twice."

When my family continued to give me blank stares, I pointed at Benji's list. "Three of the five people being harassed by Don had the opportunity to do this stuff to him. They were trying to make Amor seem like an undesirable place to build."

Instead of being excited by this revelation, my family all tilted their heads to the side in unison, their expressions perplexed.

"I don't think Cal would purposely try to hit someone with his bicycle," Lilly finally said. "He looks kinda scary, but he's probably the nicest guy in town."

Benji nodded. "Yes, but even nice people will do things to protect the ones they care about. And all five of these shop owners would have had to stand strong—together—to keep Don from taking over."

"Where does Debbie fit into all of this?" my mom asked, glancing at the list.

That was a good question. I looked to Benji, but he didn't have an answer and merely shrugged.

Lilly's eyes brightened, and she started scrolling through the pictures on her camera. "A couple days ago, I was walking around town, looking for a good shot for the magazine that hired me. Remember the one that is looking for photographs of the undiscovered parts of New Mexico?"

"I remember," I said with a smile. Ever since she'd begun to do contract work with the spaceport, she'd been getting a lot of calls like that.

Lilly continued. "Anyway, this guy walked out of Debbie's salon with a haircut that was so insane, I had to take a picture. Of course, I could never print it because I don't want people thinking it represents her usual work." She held out her camera to me. "Here, take a look for yourself."

My eyes widened when I glanced at the picture. Edna had complained about Don's terrible red hair at the town meeting, and I now understood his shaved head from when he'd shown up at my house.

The edges of Don's haircut were slanted, and pieces of long hair stuck out in patches over his head while other sections were shaved completely. It looked like a toddler had gotten ahold of a razor, and even then, I didn't think they could have done this kind of damage.

I handed the camera to Benji for him to look. "It's official, the park shop owners were definitely out to get Don."

"But if they were all in on it," Lilly said, her words slow, "does that mean..."

Her unfinished question hung in the air, and it was not one that any of us wanted to entertain, let alone answer.

"No," Benji finally said. "I don't believe that any of

them killed Don." He glanced at me. "Last night, I went to visit each of them. They confessed to making his life difficult and hoping he'd decide that Amor wasn't worth the trouble. But everything they did was harmless, meant to annoy, not injure."

"Even Cal nearly running Don over with his bike?" my mom asked.

"Cal said he was in complete control the entire time and only rode close enough to scare him. Cal wouldn't have actually hurt him."

It made sense. But there was one person who'd been left out. One person we hadn't yet discussed. I didn't even want to bring it up. Unfortunately, Flash took care of it for me.

"What about Jake Pletcher?"

My mom perked up. "What about him?"

"He owns the fifth store," Flash said. "The hardware store. So, what did he do to Don?"

An uneasy quiet settled over us.

Because it was only natural that the owner of the hardware store might visit a construction site.

And in this case, a very specific construction site.

6

I broke the silence.

"Jake wouldn't do that. And it will only add fuel to the fire if we start throwing around accusations." I winced. "Poor choice of words."

Flash snorted. "You think people would care if Jake took out the developer? They'd more likely lift him onto their shoulders and chant his name as they carried him down Main Street."

There was more truth in that statement than I liked to admit.

"Maybe Jake didn't know Don was sleeping there," Lilly suggested. "Don had a room at the hotel, and who wants to sleep on a concrete slab in the middle of a partially constructed building?"

My mom leaned back in her chair. "Makes sense. None of the other antics worked to scare Don off, so Jake felt he had to do something drastic. It would be a final symbolic gesture—something that would get the message across loud and clear that we aren't going to put up with these developers and their underhanded ways."

"Accident or not, Jake will still be tried for murder, and because he purposely set the fire, they won't let him off lightly," Lilly said. She looked to me, her eyes troubled. "Right?"

Benji held up his hands. "Hold on. We don't know for sure that Jake set that fire."

"And we can't let anyone think he did," I said. "Let the sheriff do her own investigation. She'll likely come up with the real culprit, and there's no sense putting Jake and his family through an interrogation for nothing."

Music erupted from my phone, and I slipped it out of my pocket.

Sheriff Potts.

Sometimes, I swore she had a listening device planted on me. She'd done that in the past, so it wasn't completely farfetched.

"Danielle, what can I do for you?" I said, answering the phone with a voice that was much too chipper for the situation.

"You snuck out of my crime scene awfully fast this morning. Especially for someone who was likely the last person to see the victim alive." She somehow managed to sound both stern and amused at the same time. I took that as a good sign.

"Had to get back to the office."

She chuckled. "No one intends to come in for therapy today. They're all out here snooping around and getting in my way. It's been especially bad since word got out that Don Mendes was found amongst the wreckage. Funny thing is your family has been strangely absent. Usually, your kids are the first ones I have to kick out of the crime scene."

I wasn't going to rise to the bait, not until I knew what she was really after. "Lilly has been out on a photo shoot, and Flash still has school. He's a junior in high school— can you believe it? Where does the time go?"

Flash shoved an arm over his mouth to block his laughter. He'd been begging me to let him drop out, said that school wasn't doing him any good. He had a point, considering he made more money than I did each year at his computer hacking competitions. I'd had to field several job offers already, the biggest companies in the country wanting to utilize his skills.

We'd settled on Flash graduating a year early, which meant I only had a few months left with my baby before he joined his sister in the workforce.

I didn't want to think about it.

"You know a lot more than you're telling me," the sheriff said, sidestepping my attempt at changing the topic. "How did that conversation with Don Mendes last night really go?"

I hesitated, Benji's and my family's eyes all on me as I

wound my way through a conversation they could only hear one side of. "Exactly as I said. He was acting paranoid and scared, and I asked him to come in first thing this morning so we could speak further."

A pause.

"That solidifies it, I guess. With no additional information, I have no choice but to arrest Jake Pletcher for arson and involuntary manslaughter."

My mouth opened, but I couldn't find the words. We had barely come to that conclusion ourselves, and yet Danielle had managed to process a crime scene, deal with onlookers, and still land on Jake in the same amount of time.

And with no alternative theory, I couldn't do anything about it.

"You have to go where the evidence leads you, Sheriff. You have eyewitnesses, no doubt. And physical evidence."

"Of course. Jake was seen walking around the construction site last night. Late. And alone. That wouldn't be enough to bring him in, but Lou found a lighter just outside the site. It had Jake's fingerprints on it." A long pause. "You're never this agreeable. It makes me think you're up to something."

I could see where she'd get that impression. "Don't confuse my lack of interference with agreeing with you. I don't think Jake did it—he's not the type. And he wouldn't do something like burn down a construction site. Not when he has Angel and the kids." I paused. "But with all that evidence and no other suspects, it's not like you can ignore it."

My family was now looking at me like I'd gone crazy. Giving up and staying out of the sheriff's way wasn't something I usually did. But I had no choice right now. The sheriff was right, everything pointed to Jake.

"Huh. Okay." Danielle was quiet for a moment longer. "I guess that's all I needed, for now. I'll still be processing the scene for the rest of the day and interviewing folks who might have seen something. If you come across anything—"

"I'll be sure to let you know," I finished for her.

Another pause. "Great. I'll talk to you soon, I'm sure." And then the sheriff hung up.

I lowered my phone and studied it. That had been an interesting call, mostly because she had called at all. Yes, I'd helped her on cases in the past, but this felt different. I got the impression Danielle didn't think Jake had burned down the construction site and she'd been hoping I had information that could clear him, or at least throw suspicion elsewhere. She didn't want to have to arrest Jake.

I did not envy the sheriff's job. Jake and his family were well loved in the community, and when word got out that he was in jail, Danielle was going to have her hands full. Sure, her deputy could field the phone calls, but what was he going to do about the dozens of in-person complaints she was about to be flooded with?

"What did you do that for?" my mom asked, folding

her arms across her chest. "You told the sheriff it was fine by you if she arrested Jake, who we all know is an innocent man. This is going to destroy Angel, you know. She's a good woman and a wonderful friend, but she'd make a terrible single mother." When I looked like I might protest, she held up a hand. "I know I made it look easy, raising you on my own, but the truth was that I struggled. A lot."

I had never been under the impression it had been easy. I'd seen my mom struggle—the tears. Heard the anger.

Since my divorce, I'd only gotten a small taste of what she'd gone through, and there were days when the pressures of the single-mom life almost killed me. And that was with amazing kids who were older and more independent than I had been, and a roommate and friend who helped more often than I liked to admit.

It was different.

A wave of guilt washed over me. My mom's struggles hadn't been because of my dad—not entirely, anyway. They had been because of me and my inclination to do the exact opposite of what she asked—every time.

"I didn't make it any easier," I said.

My mom walked toward me and rested a hand on my arm, kindness in her eyes. "You don't need to feel bad. Your stubbornness has made you the person you are today. Which is a pretty amazing person, by the way. You should be proud of everything you have accomplished—no apology needed."

I stared. My mother had never been one for coddling, never said things just to make me feel good. If I messed up, she made sure I knew it.

Her gaze—she was being genuine. And my heart lifted.

Tears pooled in my eyes, and I knew the exact moment she noticed the moisture, because she frowned. "My job was to make sure you survived into adulthood, relatively unscathed, and I somehow managed it. No need to get emotional."

And my mom was back. I laughed and wiped the tears from my eyes. I wouldn't have her any other way.

"Awww...you two are precious," Lilly said. "But maybe we can get back to Angel and Jake. We all know he isn't the type to go murdering someone, and yet he might be going to prison. If we don't do something and find who really started that fire, his children will be scarred for the remainder of their unhappy lives." She paused and glanced at me. "Something that could have been prevented if you'd just had a quick midnight therapy session, I might add."

Well, that took a dark turn quickly.

"I seem to remember you and Flash running outside, brandishing sports equipment that you don't know how to use," I said, raising an eyebrow. "You're saying you would have liked me to invite the guy in for a cup of tea? Maybe he could have stayed the night and borrowed your robe."

Lilly scrunched up her nose. "Why my robe?"

"Because I don't have one," Flash said, smiling, as if

this were a fact to be proud of. "After a shower, I don't wear anything at all. I just run across the hall to my room and hope no one sees."

Lilly gasped in horror and covered her eyes, as if attempting to block the scene from unfolding right there in my therapy office. "We have towels, you know."

Flash grinned wickedly. "I know."

Now he was just trying to get a reaction out of his sister. Flash had a greater inclination toward modesty than the average teenage boy and always dressed in the bathroom before leaving. Usually in the same clothes he'd been wearing for the past week, but at least he had something on.

"The point is," I said, trying to get the conversation back on track and to a place where I wasn't being blamed for sending a man to his death, "maybe the fire wasn't intentional. Maybe it was a freak accident and Lou was wrong and we have nothing to worry about because the sheriff will uncover the truth."

My mom raised her hand. "If Lou says it's arson, then it was. The man knows his fires. Someone started that blaze on purpose."

I knew she was right; it had been wishful thinking on my part. Lou was the only paid firefighter we had in town —the rest were on a volunteer basis—and he was very good at what he did. It wasn't fair to start questioning his abilities just because I didn't like where the evidence was pointing.

"But we don't have evidence it was Jake who set it," Benji said. He usually didn't interfere when my family was neck-deep in a debate—it was a risky move for anyone— and it made me sit up and take notice.

"We don't, but the sheriff does," I said. "He was seen at the scene of the crime at a time he should have been home with his family. There was also physical evidence at the scene. Fingerprints. On a lighter." My heart felt heavy in my chest as my gaze swept from Benji to Flash and Lilly, to my mom, then back to Benji. "There is a very real possibility Jake might have set that fire and accidentally killed a man when he was trying to do what he thought was the right thing—scaring away Don Mendes. And the reality of the situation is that he might be going to prison for a very a long time."

The room fell quiet.

"I know Jake," Benji finally said. "I'm in his hardware shop every single day buying supplies. We've played cards every Friday night for the past fifteen years. Long before he was married. Long before he had kids. Long before we wised up and decided to do something with our lives. And even back then, he wouldn't have done something this stupid. Jake is innocent. He didn't do it. And I'm going to prove it."

Benji then walked out the front door and didn't look back.

7

My family was quiet as we all looked at the spot where Benji had disappeared.

Normally it was my mother and the kids I had to worry about when it came to interfering in murder investigations. Benji had offered a helping hand at times, but he'd never been the instigator.

Now that it was him who was intent on proving his friend's innocence, I was unsure how I felt about this sudden change of roles.

It was weird, and confusing, and I was unsure if I was supposed to follow my boyfriend.

My conscience told me I already knew what needed to be done. Benji had always jumped in, full steam ahead, whenever I'd needed him in the past. No questions asked. And he needed me to do that for him now. That was what you did when you loved someone. Investigate murders and, against all odds, prove a man's innocence.

We'd done it before, and it was time we did it again.

"I suppose he's going to need my help," I said, moving toward the door.

"Finally," Flash shouted, excitement in his voice as he jumped from the waiting room chair he'd been lounging in. "He'll need my computer skills. You two are hopeless with technology." And he raced out the front door.

Flash just wanted an excuse to get involved in the murder investigation. I really should have put my foot down and said no, but Flash had helped so many times in the past, he knew how good he was. If I forbade him, he would just laugh at me.

Not the greatest attestation of my parenting skills, but I blamed my ex-husband for this one. My ex was the leading expert in the psychology of serial killers, and back when we'd been married, I'd lost count of how many times I had told him he shouldn't bring work home. Especially to the dinner table. Unfortunately, my kids had latched on to his stories and loved every minute of it.

My job now was to make sure my kids used their gifts for good instead of evil.

"I can help too," Lilly said, running after her brother.

My mom shot me an amused glance. "Aren't you going to try to stop this?"

"Would they listen if I tried? At nineteen years old,

Lilly is technically an adult, and Flash is graduating high school this year."

My mom moved to follow them, her hand on the door-knob. "You've been too lenient with them since the divorce. But now that the lion is out of the bag, I suppose there's no shoving it back in."

I didn't think that was how the saying went, but I understood where she was going with it. And I disagreed.

"Mom, you've literally driven the kids to crime scenes when I've told them to stay out of it. I'm not sure it's me who let the lion out."

She chuckled and opened the door. "It's a grandmother's job to spoil her grandkids. Most kids want too much sugar and junk food. Your kids like to solve murders." She glanced back. "What am I supposed to do?"

She readjusted her purse on her shoulder and walked out of the office.

"You're supposed to say *No, we can't go see the dead body today*," I yelled after her.

Not that anyone cared. I was now standing in an empty therapy office, alone, realizing that my mom had most likely left so she could join the investigation as well.

With a groan, I ran out the door, locking it behind me. My mom and the kids were already in her car, the engine running. Benji stood next to the open driver's door of his truck. "Your family has informed me that they will be joining me in my quest to prove Jake's innocence."

"Yes, they've informed me of that as well," I said.

"Sorry, I tried to stop them." Sort of. I hadn't tried very hard. More like watched them leave, then questioned all my life choices that had brought us to this point.

He smirked. "I'm sure you did."

We stared at each other a moment, his gaze questioning if I was planning on joining them as well. I'd already made up my mind before the rest of the family had jumped on board. Their decision only helped solidify it.

"First stop should probably be Jake's house," I said, moving toward the passenger door. "I know Angel is probably in no mood to answer questions, but maybe we can at least get a timeline on Jake's whereabouts last night."

Benji's eyes crinkled as he smiled, happy I was on board.

Of course I was. I trusted Benji. And if he was convinced of Jake's innocence, then I couldn't sit by and watch a family be torn apart.

"Maybe you should be the one to talk to Angel," he said, slipping into his seat. "She'll be more likely to open up to you."

I didn't know if Benji thought I could better help Angel because I was a woman or because I spent every day trying to get people to open up to me. In the end, I was just happy to help.

A little voice nagged at me, telling me I had just told the sheriff I wouldn't interfere, and here I was, sneaking out to question a murder suspect's wife.

But Benji was asking me to. And he was the love of my life.

When it came to loyalty, Benji would trump the sheriff every time.

Even so, Benji and I sat in silence for the five-minute drive. He must have known something was bothering me, because when he pulled up in front of Jake's house, he turned to me, his eyebrows knit in concern. "You don't have to do this. It was unfair of me to ask."

"You didn't ask."

Benji reached over and placed his hand on mine. "I did. Sort of. In my own way. And I don't want you to feel pressured to go inside and question a distressed woman just because we're dating, or you feel I expect it of you. I won't be upset if you feel uncomfortable getting involved with this."

I nodded slowly. "But you would like me to, wouldn't you? It would help?"

Even though Benji didn't want me to feel pressured to question Angel, I did still feel the need. If I had the opportunity to prove a man's innocence and didn't, how would I reconcile that? I wouldn't be the person I was trying so hard to be—the one who always tried to help, whatever the consequences.

Benji's gaze met mine, intense. "Yes, it would help. But regardless of your choice, I love you and plan on spending the rest of my life with you. So trust me when I say this has to be something you're okay with."

The rest of his life.

He'd been bringing up the future a lot lately. A future with me. We hadn't spoken of marriage outright, but he'd hinted at it. And every time he did, panic rose in my chest, and I felt like I was drowning.

That couldn't be a good sign.

And because I didn't want to think about what those feelings might mean, I jumped out of the truck. I'd rather question a distraught woman to help protect her future than think of my own.

"I won't be long," I said, shooting him a quick smile, and shut the door.

I ignored the curious look he gave me as I walked toward the Pletcher home.

It looked similar to most of the other homes in Amor, New Mexico, the southwest style evidenced by its stuccoed exterior, exposed beams, and arched doorway. Despite Jake running the local hardware store, it seemed he wasn't much of a landscaping guy. Prickly pear cactuses had overtaken the front yard, spilling onto the walkway, and I had to be careful as I made my way past them.

Unfortunately, the obstacles didn't end there. I soon discovered that to gain access to the house, I needed to open an ornate wooden gate that had a large Zia symbol painted in the middle, and then cross a small courtyard before I'd arrive at the front door. That felt like trespassing, though, so I scanned the gate's frame, looking for a doorbell. When I didn't find one, I peered through the gaps, wondering if Angel would mind if I let myself in.

After a brief hesitation, I slid back the latch on the gate and stepped into the courtyard. I should have listened to the first voice—the one that had said not to trespass.

Because I didn't make it more than a step or two before Angel appeared out of nowhere, a gun in her hand.

8

I had no idea where Angel had come from, but it hadn't been through the front door.

"Stop right there, Maddie," Angel warned. Her usual easy smile had been replaced by a frown of distrust.

My gaze met hers, and I lifted my hands. "I just dropped by to check on you. See if you're doing okay." I tried to keep my voice steady, but it was difficult with a gun trained on me.

Angel's hand shook so much, I was afraid she'd accidentally pull the trigger. She didn't seem like the weapon-wielding sort of woman, and I wondered if this was her first time holding a gun. That made me more nervous than if she had been a firearms expert.

What had happened in the last twenty-four hours that had elicited such an extreme change? Other than her husband being arrested for arson and murder, of course.

Movement at the window caught my eye, and I glanced over in time to see the curtain drop. Another moment later, a cat appeared behind the glass. Thank goodness her kids weren't watching this exchange.

Angel glanced over at the same time and must have seen the relief that passed across my face. "My mom picked up the twins. Just in case. Moments like this make me glad she did."

"This isn't a moment, Angel. I really am just here to see if you need anything." My arms were starting to tire, but when I began to lower my hands, Angel shoved the gun closer to me, and my hands shot back up into the air.

She shook her head. "I know how close you and the sheriff have become. And trust me, when she stopped by an hour ago, it wasn't to check on my well-being. And when Carlos Herrera stopped by a few minutes later, it definitely wasn't in the spirit of neighborly love. You'd think with all that's going on, he'd have a little more tact." Angel blew out a hard breath. "This is a wonderful town where everyone has your back—until someone spreads an unfounded rumor about you. Then they forget every time you cooked them dinner or babysat their kids or when you worked on the town event committee together. Suddenly those same people are stopping by looking for gossip. A story. They want to see what a murderer's house looks like. I suppose it would look the same as any other, but I wouldn't know. This isn't one of them."

I hoped Benji could see what was happening from the

truck and that he was on his way here to help talk Angel down. But it wasn't him who burst through the gate mere seconds later.

"Criminy, Angel," my mom shouted. "Put that gun away. You're going to hurt someone."

My breath hitched, and my life flashed before my eyes. This was the moment I was going to die because my mom didn't take a scared woman seriously.

But Angel was so startled by my mom's outburst, she didn't shoot anyone. Instead, she dropped the gun, looking shocked she'd even been holding it. "I'm sorry," she said, staring at it before collapsing onto the ground, sobs racking her body. "It's just, there have been so many phone calls and random people showing up at the house, some thanking me for Jake's selfless service in ridding the town of that developer. Others were...not so friendly. I don't know how everyone found out so quickly. The sheriff only arrested Jake an hour ago."

That did seem quick, even by Amor's standards. But everyone had been out to see the construction site, so maybe this was just the next stop on their tour.

I was about to say something comforting—I hadn't decided what yet, but it would certainly help Angel feel better about the situation, I was sure of it—when Benji ran into the courtyard. His breaths came out as gasps.

"Phone call.... CJ.... burst pipe... your kids... Carlos..."

The pieces of this particular puzzle weren't coming together easily for me, but I thought I understood enough to make a wild conjecture. "CJ has a burst pipe at the auto shop and called to see if you could fix it. And you want to take my kids along for the ride to keep them out of trouble?"

Benji gave a vigorous shake of his head and sucked in a long breath before a second attempt at communication. "You're right about CJ's burst pipe, but I can't go deal with that right now. I told him to shut off the water and I'll stop by first thing in the morning. While I was on the phone, I noticed Carlos Herrera at the end of the street, watching Jake and Angel's house. The kids thought he was acting suspicious and wanted to confront him."

"Told you he was up to something," Angel said, giving me a knowing look.

"I tried to catch up with Flash and Lilly," Benji said after pulling in another long breath. "But Carlos disappeared around the corner, and so did they. By the time I reached the end of this street, the three of them were gone."

Angel was still nodding, like she could have told us something like this would happen. I buried my head in my hands, reminding myself that Carlos Herrera wasn't a bad guy. More like a nosy one, but otherwise harmless.

Flash and Lilly would play spy for a little while, get bored, and they'd wander on back.

"Thanks for trying," I told him, grateful. That was one of the things I loved most about Benji. He'd met my kids for the first time three years earlier, but from that first day, he'd looked out for them. Always treated them as his own. Their dad was too busy for that kind of stuff, and I was eternally grateful they had a positive male role model.

My mom glared at Angel with squinted eyes, like she was afraid if she took her gaze off her, Angel would grab the gun again. "Want me to go round them up?" she asked me.

I weighed the pros and cons. Sending my mom after the kids would help get her out of the way for a bit while Benji and I talked with Angel, as well as ease my mind that they were okay. They'd be offended I didn't trust them enough to take care of themselves, but what if Carlos wasn't as harmless as he'd always appeared?

And everyone in town knew better than to mess with my mom.

"That would be great. Thank you."

My mom hesitated before turning to me and lowering her voice. "You going to be okay with her? Angel isn't the type to brandish a weapon and probably doesn't even know how to use it, but this sudden burst of violence means she might have lost her mind, and anything is possible at this point."

"We'll be fine," I told her with a smile, just in case Angel was watching. In reality, I had no idea what to expect. This day had already taken a sharp turn from what I'd had in mind, though I doubted it could get any worse.

My mom nodded slowly. "Well, call if you need anything." She walked out the gate, but not without a couple of backward glances. It was nice to see how much she worried.

"We should probably head out too," Benji said, nodding toward his truck.

That wasn't the plan. I could still talk to Angel. Get her to confide. Now that the gun wasn't in play anymore, I felt like we'd gained a little of her trust. "Why don't you start the truck, and I'll be there in a minute." I gave him a smile that said *I love you. I know what I'm doing. Please go along with it.*

Benji returned my smile, but it was accompanied by a determined gaze. "We don't want to be late for our dinner date in the city."

He knew how much I hated being late for anything. However, Benji and I didn't have a date in the city. He was trying to move me along, which I didn't understand. It was because of him that I was here in the first place.

"Darling," I said through a tight smile, "I think you're mistaken. Our reservations are for tomorrow evening."

"I changed them." Benji was no longer even pretending to smile. This was such a deviation from his usual easy-going self that I felt I had no choice but to follow his lead and head back to the truck, empty-handed.

After a quick goodbye to Angel, and an even quicker apology from her for threatening to shoot me, Benji and I got in the truck.

"What was that about?" I asked as soon as he pulled away from the curb. "You wanted info. She was starting to trust that I didn't have ulterior motives. I could have gotten something."

Benji's gaze didn't stray from the road in front of us. "Yes, but how quickly would she have changed her mind if you started grilling her about Jake?" He hesitated. "I saw the gun on the ground. I didn't even know they owned one. And if anything were to happen to you..."

I placed a hand on his sleeve. "It didn't. I told her I was there to check in on her. Make sure she was doing okay."

"And is she doing okay?" Benji asked, glancing at me.

I released a heavy sigh. "No. She's not. Honestly, we probably should have taken the gun with us. She's in panic mode, not knowing what's going on or who to trust."

I sat back in my seat, frustrated with myself. Benji had been right to not question Angel any further. I had completely misread the situation and might have gotten us into worse trouble.

Benji glanced at me. "There's something else." Even though we were the only ones in the truck, his voice had dropped to just above a whisper.

My heart immediately picked up its pace, and I tried to remain calm. "What?"

"It's not evidence, but it at least presents reasonable doubt." He nodded to his phone on the center console between us. "Look at the last picture on there."

I held up his phone so he could punch in his password, but then was confused when I saw the picture that popped up.

It was a pile of junk that had been on the Pletchers' front porch.

"I don't get it," I said, glancing over at him as he rounded the corner toward my house. "It's a bunch of stuff that looks like it could be sold at a yard sale." I paused. "No, it's not even good enough for that. It's trash."

Benji motioned to the phone impatiently. "What's in the pile?"

I used my fingers to zoom in on the screen. "Old wooden planks, broken toys, empty milk jugs and... lighters." Not just one or two, more like ten of them. A couple were still in the original packaging, but the rest were stacked in a haphazard pile on the ground. Lighters were like pens. You knew you had one somewhere, but when you couldn't find it, you'd buy another. The process continued until you realized you had twenty half-used pens, or lighters in this case.

"And those lighters likely all have one thing we can use to free Jake."

I nodded in understanding. "They will all have his fingerprints on them."

9

"We have to talk to Angel," I said. "Ask her who might have had access to these lighters. If we can send the sheriff this picture and a few names to look into, then Jake's not the only suspect anymore." I craned my neck to look behind us, as if that would make Benji turn the truck around and drive back to the Pletcher house.

He didn't turn around and gave no indication he planned to. "Did you notice anything odd about Angel's behavior?"

My gaze whipped back to him. "You mean besides pulling a gun on me? Nope, not a thing." Benji caught the sarcasm, and his lips pursed. I placed my hand on his. "I'm sorry. You've been right about everything, every step of the way on this. I'm just not used to..." I tried to find the words.

"Not used to following someone else's lead?" he asked,

shooting me a small smile. "You're a single mom, and you own your own business. You've had to lead the charge the last few years. I get it. But you're not alone anymore. We're a team. And I need you to trust me. Jake is my friend, and my only goal is to prove he didn't burn down the construction site."

A team. I liked the sound of that.

"All right. Tell me more about Angel."

Benji visibly relaxed as he pulled up in front of my house. My mom hadn't returned yet, but she hadn't left Angel's house all that long ago.

"Angel and Jake are the calmest people I've ever met. When we get together for cards at their house, they work together seamlessly to put the kids in bed and keep the chaos at a minimum. Angel even joins in on our games. There couldn't be a more perfect couple.

"But today—she was on edge. Paranoid. It either means she suspects someone close to them had something to do with the fire and she doesn't know who to trust, or—"

I held up a hand to stop his thoughts mid-track. "If you're about to tell me that Angel could have burned down the construction site, don't. She didn't do it."

Benji released a sigh. "I know." He looked sad at the thought, which didn't make any sense, though I thought I understood why.

"If Angel and Jake didn't start the fire, it would need to either be someone Jake gave a lighter to or someone who snatched it off their porch," I said. "But because of the gated courtyard, the pile of junk is hidden from view. Whoever set Jake up had access to the house."

He nodded slowly. "Like maybe someone in our Friday night card group. And I think Angel figured that out, which was why when she saw you, who happen to be dating me, she immediately went on the defensive."

As horrible as it would be if Angel had set that fire, the idea that one of one of Jake's friends could have set him up to take the fall for a murder he didn't commit almost felt like a worse betrayal. It wasn't, of course. But it felt like it. Because the same group of men had been playing cards every Friday night for the past fifteen years. Twice as long as Angel and Jake had been married.

"I know that Cal and Lou are in your Friday night group," I said slowly. "We can rule Lou out, though. Whoever heard of a firefighter who starts fires?" Now that I thought about it, there had been quite a few in the news over the years. But Lou was different. I wasn't willing to consider that possibility.

Of course, I didn't want to consider Cal capable, either. I tried not to think about the fact that he had tried to scare Don Mendes with his bicycle, because it wasn't the same thing. Arson and murder were in a league of their own, no matter how accidental they may have been.

The thought must have also crossed Benji's mind because he said, "I know Cal looks like he's capable of doing shady stuff, and he's strong enough to bench press me and you at the same time. But he's a gentle giant, I promise."

"Okay, so who else comes to game night?" I asked. "Anyone with motive?"

"Buck is the only other one. It's always been just the five of us."

I gave a slow nod. "That's quite the game night group you have there. Three of your guys own small shops that Don wanted to buy out—Cal with the bike shop, Buck with his electronics repair place, and Jake with the hardware shop. Then you have Lou, the town firefighter, when arson was what killed Don."

I leaned my head on Benji's shoulder. "And then there's you."

Benji kissed the top of my head. "I don't like what these developers have done to our town—how they've turned Amor into their own personal playground and twisted everything good about us into something unrecognizable." He used his free hand to massage his forehead. I could relate—I felt a headache coming on too.

"There are a lot of people who are unhappy with them," I said. "And even good people can do awful things when they're pushed beyond their limits." I'd seen a lot of that over the last few years. More than I liked.

"But these are my guys," Benji said. "My people. We've been through everything together. For some of them, it's been marriage and babies. For others, things like death and loneliness."

Sometimes I forgot that Benji had been engaged at one time. And that she had been cruelly taken from him, through no fault of either of them. I also knew that a scar like that would never go away. Not for him.

"You've trusted each other, bonded on the deepest levels, which means you also feel responsible to protect each other." I straightened, and our gazes met. "You don't have to go any further with this investigation. The sheriff doesn't even know you've been asking around, trying to make the puzzle pieces fit. You can walk away, and no one will be the wiser."

I knew that wouldn't be enough for Benji. Not at this point. But I also wanted him to know there was always another option. That if he went any further with this, it was his choice. Because investigating your own friends—I wouldn't wish that on anyone. Unfortunately for him, Benji had always been a road-less-traveled kind of guy. And I doubted this would be any different.

"I can't walk away," he whispered.

I kissed him. "I know."

We were silent for a moment as Benji rubbed his thumb over my knuckles. "So, now what?"

"Now..." I glanced around, realizing my mom and the kids were taking far too long to return. "We find out why my family isn't back yet."

When my kids had taken off, I hadn't been worried. They had decided to follow an overzealous member of town council. It had been something to occupy their time while I interviewed Angel. But now?

Now I wondered if Angel had every right to be paranoid.

What if Carlos had had access to those lighters and we didn't realize it? Maybe that had been why he'd visited Angel so soon after Jake's arrest. To make sure he hadn't left behind any evidence.

And now I was worried.

M y mom's phone rang far too many times. Eventually, it went to voicemail. Lilly's phone did the same, as did Flash's.

"They're not picking up," I said, turning my panicked gaze on Benji. "They've been gone too long, and now they're not answering."

"I know Carlos. He wouldn't do anything to your family." It was his eyes that gave him away. He didn't want to believe it of Carlos, but he was no longer as certain as he once had been.

"I'm calling Danielle." I found the sheriff's number in my phone's contacts list, but before I could press the green call icon, my mom's car turned onto the street and parked directly behind Benji's truck.

My panic turned to relief when she and the kids got out, completely unscathed. "I was about to call the sheriff and tell her to forget about her murder investigation, that she had three missing persons on her hands," I said, walking quickly toward my mom, who had bent over to pull something from the car.

She paused and glanced over her shoulder. "Why would you do a silly thing like that?"

I balked. "Maybe because you should have been home by now, and the last time I saw you, you were leaving to find my kids, who were following a potential murder suspect."

She laughed as she pulled a large bag from the back seat. "A bit dramatic, aren't you? I would hardly say that Carlos is a murder suspect. And rather than confronting him for being a nosy gossip, we decided it would be advantageous to follow him instead. Of course, it ended up being far more boring than we'd anticipated, so we stopped by the diner to pick up food for dinner." She paused as she lifted the bag into the air. "You're welcome."

I forced myself to pull in a long breath. She didn't know I suspected Carlos might have had something to do with the construction site fire. And she had picked up dinner, which meant I didn't have to cook.

"Thank you, Mom," I said, meaning it. "It's been a long, stressful day, and I really appreciate you going to the trouble."

Her eyes lit up. "You're welcome." Her gaze landed somewhere over my shoulder. "Next time if you want us to follow someone, though, it should be Edna. She knows everything that goes on in this town, and some of what happens in the next town over."

I glanced behind me to see Edna power walking up her driveway and into her house. If power walking ever returned as an Olympic sport, I had no doubt she'd take home the gold. Sometimes it seemed it was all she did.

I hadn't asked my family to follow anyone—that had been done of their own accord—but my mom gave me a knowing look, like I should consider pumping Edna for information.

"Talking to Edna is actually a pretty good idea," I said.

"Of course it is," my mom said. "And maybe while you're over there, you can suggest she spend less time worrying about others and more time worrying about the state of her house. Do you see the paint splattered all over her driveway from those silly ceramic frogs she paints? The least she could do is clean up occasionally."

My mom then hobbled inside, the heavy bag of food throwing her off balance as she lugged it along. The kids weren't so quick to follow, and considering how much Flash loved food, it meant something was wrong.

"What happened?" I asked them as they walked toward the house at the speed of a funeral march. Both stopped mid-step, as if they'd been waiting for me to ask.

"Mr. Herrera stopped by four or five houses." Lilly lifted her camera. "We took pictures. He was acting super sketchy the whole time, his eyes jumping everywhere, like he was worried he was being followed."

"Which he was," Flash added, "so I guess he had every right to be paranoid."

Lilly shot her brother an annoyed look. "Anyway, the first stop he made was to the mayor's house, which was interesting. He wasn't there, of course, midday on a Tuesday. Mr. Herrera seemed annoyed that it was only Katie and their daughter who were home."

"Who else did he visit?" Benji asked, his tone abrupt. "And I'd like to see the pictures, please."

The kids weren't used to Benji using that tone with them, and they exchanged raised eyebrows.

"I don't know," Lilly said slowly. "Didn't recognize the houses, and no one else answered their doors. Everyone's at work, probably, but Carlos was acting all panicky, like he'd expected them to be there."

Benji flipped through the pictures, his eyebrows scrunching up further with each one. "It's all of them," he said. "He visited Buck, Lou, and Cal." He glanced up at me. "But why?"

"Have you two figured out something?" Flash asked, looking between us. "Because Benji is acting like a crazy person, which isn't exactly his MO. That's more mom's thing."

I should have been offended at that, but Flash was right. For a therapist, I was a bit more off my rocker than the average person.

"Don't you worry about a thing," I said with what was, hopefully, a reassuring smile. "Carlos probably just wants to be a part of their Friday night guys' group. Should be an interesting one this week."

Lilly tilted her head to the side. "But don't they get together every Friday?"

"Yeah, they do." I tried to keep my smile from dipping.

She watched me, her gaze laser focused, as she asked, "And they've been getting together every Friday for like ever. So, why is Benji excited for this one in particular? Is it someone's birthday? Does he have a big announcement to make?" Her eyes widened, and her voice dropped to a whisper. "Are you pregnant?"

Heat rushed into my face, and I wanted to melt into the ground. "No, of course not," I sputtered. "I'm too old for something like that."

Lilly shook her head, now looking convinced that that was the reason Benji was acting weird. "No, you're only forty-three, and I've read that unless you've gone through menopause, you can successfully have babies into your mid to late forties. It's not as common, but still completely possible. Have you gone through menopause yet? I'm assuming not because you made a quick run to the market for tampons last month."

Flash now had his hands over his ears, humming, but Benji was leaning in, looking thoroughly amused.

How this conversation had derailed so quickly I would never know. "No, I have not gone through menopause," I said, my voice low and my words quick. I kept my back to

Benji. "But I am not pregnant, and this conversation is never happening again. Got it?"

Lilly frowned, like she had been certain she'd solved the mystery. "No offense, but you two aren't the most exciting people in town. If you're not pregnant, the only other announcement that would be excitement worthy would be...an engagement." She hopped from foot to foot and squealed. "You two are getting married. It's about time too."

Flash removed his hands from his ears. "You're getting married?" He raised his hand to high-five Benji. "Right on."

"Did I hear someone say something about a wedding?" my mom called, poking her head out the front door. That woman could hear a roadrunner a mile away. Her hearing was very selective, though, and she usually chose not to use it. Of course, now would be the time she decided to turn it on. "The least you could have done is wait until you were inside. Now gossiping Edna knows, and once again, I'm the last to find out."

This was getting out of hand. "No one is pregnant, and no one is getting married," I half-yelled in frustration. "We think one of Benji's game night friends set Jake up to take the fall for Don's murder. That's all. There is no big announcement."

I realized a moment too late that that had not come out like I had intended. At all. Four faces were staring at me. Flash and Lilly looked like they were in shock. My mom seemed equally taken aback. But it was Benji's expression that made me wish I could rewind time. The pain in his eyes made my heart hurt.

"Benji, I didn't mean—"

The damage had been done. He gave me a single nod and then jumped back into the truck and drove away.

I stood on the sidewalk, my gaze on the spot where Benji's truck had disappeared around a corner, hoping against hope it would reappear. It never did.

"Mom," Lilly said, touching my sleeve.

I wiped moisture from my eyes and turned back to see we were alone. My mom and Flash had gone inside at some point, and I'd not noticed.

"I better get dinner on," I said, turning back toward the house.

Lilly didn't move. "Grandma picked up food from the diner, remember?" She paused. "Mom, do you not want to marry Benji?"

Fear washed over me. Disappointment. Regret.

The feelings had nothing to do with Benji and everything with how my marriage had ended four years earlier.

"I don't know," I said, wanting to be honest with her. She was old enough to have adult conversations, even if they were hard. "Marriage scares me. I mean, everything is so good now, what if signing that piece of paper changes it? What if marrying Benji ends the same way my marriage to your dad did?"

Lilly held up a finger. "For starters, Benji is nothing like

Dad. All Dad cares about is his work. Benji on the other hand...yeah, he works hard. But at the end of the day, you come first. So do Flash and I. We know that if we need anything, he'll be there. Heck, even Jake, who is sitting in the sheriff's cell at Town Hall right now, can count on Benji. Because he is loyal and kind and the best friend anyone could ever ask for." She paused. "Is that not enough?"

Ouch.

I knew Lilly hadn't meant to hurt me. She was nothing but genuine. But it still felt like a dagger had been thrust through my heart.

Because she was right. I would never find another Benji, and I didn't want to. He was my person. And I had managed to mess that up in a matter of seconds. A thoughtless comment said out of frustration.

I had a feeling that words weren't what would fix things right now. Words were easy—too easy, as I was finding out. What I needed to do was show him how much I cared about him. And that meant helping him prove Jake's innocence. He wasn't going to have to do this alone.

I didn't want him to ever have to do anything alone again.

Turning to Lilly, I pulled her into a hug. "Thank you." When I pulled back, an idea was already forming. "I believe we need to express our sympathy to Benji's friends. They must all be having a tough time of it right now. And nothing says *I'm sorry your friend has been accused of murder, if you need a listening ear, I'd love to help* more than huevos rancheros."

Lilly raised an eyebrow. "We're going to deliver dinner to all the murder suspects?"

I smiled and gave a quick nod. "Yes. But it will have to wait until tomorrow. We need to give them time to stew. The suspects, not the food," I added, as if there had been a chance of confusion. "That and I need to go to the market. We're going to need a lot of green chile."

11

"Do you really feel this is the best way to go about it?" Lilly asked, struggling under the weight of disposable trays full of corn tortillas and fried eggs. Her brother was carrying plastic containers full of green chile sauce, and I was attempting to figure out a way to place them in the trunk of the car without spilling them all over everything.

Flash handed me one of his containers. "Of course this is the best way. Food always opens doors and gets people talking. Not only that, but this means we get to have huevos rancheros for dinner too. She never cooks this good when it's just us."

I threw an amused glance over my shoulder. "I cook all the time now. Do you remember when I worked at the university? Getting a home-cooked meal was something that happened on Thanksgiving and Christmas Eve. And not always then."

"You do cook," Flash conceded. "But not huevos rancheros."

It wasn't until all the food was in the back of the car and I had slammed the trunk closed that I began to second guess my decision. Maybe Lilly was right. Was it weird that I was showing up at their houses with dinner? Maybe I should have done something simpler. Like cookies.

Too late now.

I gave my kids a small wave and opened the driver's side door. "If I'm not back in two hours, I want you to call the sheriff. And Benji. And whoever else will listen to you. Explain why I was driving all over town with a bunch of tortillas and eggs."

"You forgot the cheese in the fridge," Flash said. "And Grandma wanted to come with you. Give me one minute." And then he ran back inside as quickly as his name implied.

Oh, no. Not my mom. I would be forever grateful for her help in making all these trays of food, but her presence wasn't exactly conducive to discreet questioning of murder suspects.

"You also forgot me," Benji said.

His sudden appearance startled me, and I jumped, hitting my knee on the car door. "Ow." I froze, my gaze moving to where Benji stood next to my car. "I would have called," I said slowly. "But I thought... Well, I figured... And then..."

Benji's lips quirked up into a smile as I struggled to find the words to tell him I knew I had hurt him, and I was sorry, and could he ever forgive me?

"It's okay," he said. "Lilly called and told me what you were up to. She thought I'd like to maybe stop you from doing something crazy." I opened my mouth to protest, but he continued. "I actually think dinner is a good idea, and I'd like to join you."

Relief flooded through me. "You would?"

"Of course. How would it look if my girlfriend showed up, alone, to bring all these single men food? They might mistake your intentions."

Heat rushed into my cheeks. I hadn't thought of that.

Benji slid into the passenger seat just as my mom came bustling out of the house, her purse slung over one shoulder.

I tried to look as sorry as I could when I told her I needed her home with the kids and I was going to be delivering the food with Benji instead.

Her gaze bounced between us, as if she was trying to ascertain whether I was kidding.

"I really am sorry." I then lowered my voice, hoping only she could hear me. "The real reason is that I could use another set of eyes on the kids. They are planning on cooking up a batch of tortillas for our own dinner, and they are more likely to burn the house down if you're not here."

Both Lilly and Flash turned accusatory gazes on me; my voice had carried more than I'd realized. I didn't blame them for being annoyed. They had learned how to make homemade tortillas from their grandma and were actually pretty good cooks. I mouthed *sorry*, hoping they knew what my true intention had been and that insulting their cooking skills had not been it. They responded with an amused eye roll, so it seemed all was forgiven.

My mom, however, gave an understanding nod. "You're right. A grandma's job isn't always glamorous, but it keeps the world going round. Our town can't handle any more fires right now. Mark my words, if I had been at that construction site, those flames would have been out before they'd had the chance to burn."

Whatever high opinion my mom had of herself, I was grateful for it. Because she was right. As much as she drove me crazy, when I had moved back to my hometown, she had jumped right in to help my family. If I ever needed anything, I knew she would be there. She had literally kept my world turning.

SILENCE. It had settled over Benji and me the moment I'd pulled away from the house and continued as I drove toward Main Street. I felt like I should be the one responsible for avoiding an awkward ride, but thus far, I was terrible at it.

I had no idea what to say. How could I address the subject of our relationship and the things I'd said about marriage when it wasn't a topic we'd ever discussed? Marriage was something Benji, my family, and the rest of the town just assumed would happen. Before I could form my thoughts enough to approach the subject, though, Benji broke the silence.

"What's our first stop?" he asked as I took a left by Debbie's hair salon.

I glanced at the address on my phone and made another right. "I thought maybe we'd see Buck first. He's always the first to close up shop and should be home by now."

"Good call."

Silence fell over us again.

"I'm sorry," we simultaneously said, then we both gave a nervous laugh and were quiet, wondering who should speak first. I wanted it to be me.

"I really am sorry for my outburst yesterday," I said. "I didn't mean it the way it came out. I was just so frustrated with my family…"

Benji was already shaking his head. "No, you don't need to be sorry. I've been pushing you to be ready for something you're obviously not. Whenever I bring up our future, you get really quiet, and I've ignored it. Pretended like you were just tired that day or maybe you didn't hear me."

I compared the address on my phone to an adobe-style house on our left and pulled the car over, putting it in park. "I do want a future with you, Benji. I do. But you need to understand that it's scary for me. I was married for a long time, and it didn't end well."

Benji's lips dipped into a frown. "Yeah, I know. Hard things happen. I was engaged for a long time, and that didn't end well either." He released a sigh and combed his fingers through his hair, as if buying time to find the right words. "All I'm saying is if you don't want to get married, that's fine. If you want to date forever until we're seventy, I'll figure out a way to deal with it. But we can't let our pasts dictate our future."

Pressure settled on my chest. I squeezed my eyes shut and forced deep breaths. I was realizing it wasn't the marriage certificate that was causing all this anxiety. It was the thought of committing the rest of my life to another person, no matter how wonderful he was.

"No, we can't," I agreed. I opened my eyes. "But what would our future even look like? You want to live and die in Amor, but I'm not sure I want to stay here forever. There might be other adventures I want to explore. Maybe I'll eventually want to return to teaching at the academic level. What then?"

Benji reached over and placed a hand on mine. "Then maybe we leave Amor. I don't know. The thing is, you can come up with all the hypothetical situations you want, and there will always be what-ifs. But if you're with the person you love, none of them matter. You figure it out as you go along. Together."

And then he stepped out of the car and waited for me to open the trunk.

I pulled the lever and the trunk lid popped up, but I didn't immediately get out of the car. I wished I could see things the way Benji did. It would be so nice. So much easier. But I was a planner. I was wired to look twenty years into the future. Benji and I—we had different goals. Different dreams.

We loved each other. He loved my family.

But was that enough?

BENJI and I carried the trays, sauces, and cheese up to Buck's house, acting like the serious conversation in the car hadn't just happened. The plan was that Buck would invite us to place the food on the counter, and once inside, we could strike up a conversation.

What we hadn't expected was for Cal to open the door. Or for the rest of the Friday night gang to be there.

If Benji was surprised to see everyone there, and not to have been invited, he didn't show it. He merely grinned and said, "We heard there was a party and brought food. Huevos rancheros sound good to everyone?"

I was impressed with how smoothly he had pulled that

out and tried not to laugh at Cal's surprised expression at seeing us there.

Cal wasn't able to think of a good reason not to invite us in, so he opened the door wider, and we paraded past him, Buck, and Lou.

"We were...just coming up with ways we could help Angel while the sheriff is figuring stuff out with Jake," Buck said, obviously flustered and looking guilty at being caught.

Benji played off it perfectly, not sounding like he was in the least bit bothered. "Great."

And then he went out to the car for the rest of the food since we would no longer need to make additional stops.

"We checked in on Angel yesterday," I said nonchalantly as I took tinfoil off the tortillas and eggs. "She certainly could use the support. What ideas have you come up with so far?"

They all looked at each other, not saying anything.

I shouldn't have enjoyed their discomfort, but I found it very satisfying. I didn't like being lied to. Or when Benji's best friends had secret meetings where Benji was excluded. I took it as a personal offense.

"We..." Cal started, but didn't get any further than that. Considering he was such a large man, he seemed awfully small in that moment. Even his tattoos seemed to have faded, and it strengthened my resolve.

I turned quickly to them, like I'd just come up with a brilliant idea. "I know what would really help Angel out.

You could babysit the twins a couple hours each day so she can go visit Jake."

I doubted they knew the twins were with Angel's mom, and considering that all these men were bachelors, I found the idea hilarious.

Not surprisingly, none of the men seemed to love it.

"You know, we'll put that on the list," Buck said, as if he was considering it. "I'm sure Angel would love that."

I had to hold back a laugh. Buck was the least likely to know how to change a diaper or what to do with an active toddler. He was a bachelor by choice and went out with a different woman every week. It was one of the main reasons he was the first of his friends to close his shop each evening.

I held up a finger. "You know what would really help her, though?" I paused for dramatic effect. "If we managed to figure out who framed Jake. I bet she'd really like that."

12

I hadn't intended on throwing that out there. Accusing your friends of murder needed finesse. A skilled hand. And of course, huevos rancheros. Otherwise, everyone would be scared off and I'd be left with nothing, exactly as had happened to the sheriff.

Watching everyone pretend how much they cared about Jake and his family, though, made my instincts scream that these men needed the exact opposite. A firm hand. The element of surprise. And for them to turn on each other.

Benji walked in, two trays piled and the green chile sauce sitting precariously on top. He noticed the shocked expressions on his friends, all staring at me, and knew exactly what I'd done.

"Can I talk to you for a minute?" he murmured to me as he set the food on the counter.

I gave a discreet shake of my head.

Buck was the first to recover from his surprise. He pretended my words hadn't affected him in the least and picked up a paper plate, placing a tortilla on it. He wasn't going to let anything get in the way of good food. And it really was delicious. I'd taste tested it before we'd left.

Buck threw a glance my way after placing an egg on the tortilla. "You really think someone framed Jake?" He looked eager, like he hoped it was true.

I gave a small nod. "Yes, I do."

He released a long sigh. "That's a relief. And here we were—"

"Buck," Cal barked. The town's favorite tattooed bike shop owner no longer looked so friendly. His eyebrows pulled down until they touched, and he glared at his friend. "Stop talking." He looked to Benji, then dropped his gaze.

So, that was why Benji hadn't been invited. They didn't trust him. That didn't make sense, though. They'd been friends since high school.

Unless it wasn't him they didn't trust—it was me.

Looking around the group, I suddenly had doubts about my ability to help in this situation. Maybe I was more of a hindrance, and I should have left Benji to his own devices.

But the way Buck had seemed so relieved when I'd declared that someone had framed Jake—

"That's why you're all here," I said, realization settling

in. "You're trying to figure out how you can help Jake. Not because you believe him innocent. You think he did it."

Benji gaped in surprise, and he spun to Lou. "You think Jake started that fire?"

Lou's gaze dropped. "Jake's a good guy, and it would be wonderful if he were innocent. But Don Mendes and his company were more of a threat to Jake and his family than anyone else here. Don thought if he could get Jake to sell, Jake would convince the rest of the Parkside shops to sell as well."

"Why Jake?" I asked. "Why not Cal or Buck or Debbie?"

Lou threw a glance my way. "When you're single, you can take more risks. But kids—they change everything. You know that. And Don knew all the right buttons to push. Or the wrong ones, as it were. His plan was to invoke fear and panic so that folks would make the decision he was pushing them toward. But with Jake—he pushed too hard." Lou shrugged. "Jake was trying to protect his family, and he made a mistake in the heat of the moment. But he shouldn't be punished for murder. How was he supposed to know that Don was sleeping in there? When I think of Angel and the twins..." His voice hitched, and he stopped talking.

That was probably wise, considering the situation.

Benji spoke up for the first time since he'd returned with the food. His voice was level, but he was straining to remain calm. "You kept something like this from me?

You've been my friends for over two decades. And now you don't trust me. I don't understand when that happened."

"It's not you," I said. "They're afraid I'll go to the sheriff."

Lou hesitated, but then nodded. "We know how close you two are."

I held up a hand as if I was swearing an oath in court. "I promise I'm not going to say anything. If there is a way to help Jake, you need to find it."

I emphasized that *they* needed to find it, as if I was taking myself out of the equation. Especially because I wasn't as convinced as they were of Jake's guilt. When I had seen Jake and Angel the night of the town meeting, they hadn't seemed the least bit interested in attending. If they were that concerned about Don Mendes, I'd think at least one of them would have wanted to contribute to the discussion. On the contrary, they'd seemed at ease, enjoying an evening family walk, not at all distressed like Lou made it sound.

But I couldn't voice any of that. For one, despite my assurances, I knew that not one of these men trusted me any more than they had ten minutes ago. And two, I was still fairly certain that at least one of these men was responsible for framing their friend.

If I was going to figure out which it was, I needed to ensure they saw me as someone who was going to stay out of their way.

Considering my track record, that was going to be tricky.

BENJI and I hadn't even reached my front door when my mom burst out of it.

"So, who did it?" she asked. The need to be the first to know before anyone else in town gleamed in her eyes.

"Don't know," I said, pushing past her into the house.

Of course she wasn't satisfied with that answer. "Oh, come on. We both know you do." She turned to Benji. "Who did it? Was it Cal? It's all those tattoos. They do something to a person."

Benji gave her a placating smile, but it couldn't hide the sadness in his eyes. "We honestly don't know. My friends all think Jake is guilty. Or at least that's what they're saying. To them, it's not a matter of who did it but how they can help get Jake's charges reduced and who is going to help take care of Angel and the kids while it's all getting sorted."

My mom harrumphed as she followed us inside. "Anyone who knows Jake and Angel knows they wouldn't go around burning down buildings, let alone leave evidence that they did it."

She had a point. No one knew Angel and Jake better than Benji and those three men. So why were they so convinced that he was guilty?

"What about the eyewitness?" I asked. "Do we know

who it could have been? Maybe we can get more details. It was at night, so to identify Jake as the person walking around the construction site, the witness must have stopped and talked to him. Otherwise, he's an average man with an average build and no discernible features who's shrouded in darkness."

"I haven't heard anything," Benji said. "But maybe a call to the sheriff could remedy that."

I raised an eyebrow. "There's no way I can call Danielle and get information from her. I already told her I'm not interfering in the case, and if she knows we're snooping around, she's going to put a quick stop to it."

"Angel might know," my mom offered. "I know she gave you a less than ideal welcome yesterday, but if she knows you're trying to help, maybe she'd be willing to give you a little more to go on."

That wasn't a terrible idea, though I didn't love the thought of returning when I knew she still had that gun.

I looked to Benji for guidance. These were his friends, after all, and I may have already made a mess of things.

"What do you think?" I asked, following him into the dining room. "Do we dare try again?"

Benji slid into a chair at the table and leaned back, a thoughtful expression on his face. "Yes, I think so," he said. "Angel is alone and scared and doesn't know who she can trust. She needs someone on her side, and I'm hoping we can convince her that we can be an advocate for her."

It was the alone and scared part that made me nervous. She didn't seem to handle them very well.

"Considering what happened last time, I'd suggest we call first," I told Benji, kissing the top of his head, then moved into the connected kitchen to make some huevos rancheros of our own.

"I think that's a good idea," my mom piped up from the other room. "I won't be there to save you from Angel's erratic behavior this time."

The fact that my mother was agreeing with me was shocking, but even more surprising was that she wasn't jumping in the car, demanding to come along.

Benji and I shared confused looks, and my mom peeked her head around the corner. "I'll take it by your stunned silence that you expected to have me as backup, but it's bingo night at the library. Last time I won a free Harry Potter T-shirt and movie poster. Can't break my lucky winning streak."

I wondered how long those had been tucked away in the library's storage room before making their appearance at bingo night. Close to two decades, I'd bet. It was funny that my mom was acting like she'd won the jackpot, considering she had immediately given the items to Flash, who had given them to Lilly, who had given them to Debbie, who had been the only one thrilled to receive them. Debbie had said she was going to hang the poster in her salon, so hopefully my mom wouldn't notice the next time she went in for a haircut.

"It's all right. I understand," I said. "And I'm sure you'll come back with something even bigger and better tonight."

She gave me a large smile, like she was up to something. "You can count on it." And then she disappeared out the front door without another word.

"What do you think that's about?" I asked, turning to Benji.

Without missing a beat, he said, "Cheating."

"How can you cheat at bingo? Every card is randomized, and they spin that ball cage, making the drawing of numbers random as well."

"Knowing your mom, she's found a way."

I was sure there was some truth to that.

"She bribes Mr. Herrera," a voice called down the stairs. Flash materialized at the top. "He's town council's official bingo caller. Grandma promises him a loaf of banana nut bread for every time she wins. I think she's had to make him around six loaves now."

I blinked. "What? That's impossible."

"No, they have a good system down. If she has one number left on her card, she texts him and he pretends to pull out that exact one, regardless of what the number on the ball actually is. The bingo round is over once someone wins, and everyone clears their boards, so no one is any the wiser. She just makes sure to not win too often." Flash said it so matter-of-factly, like it was the most natural thing in the world.

"Carlos must really love 'her banana bread," I said, shaking my head and glancing up at Flash. "She told you all of this?"

"Sometimes Grandma uses me as the middleman and pays me to text messages to Mr. Herrera. She doesn't want to leave a trail. People might be upset if they found out, you know."

I rubbed my temples, attempting to make sense of what my son was telling me. "Your grandma pays you to pass messages to Carlos Herrera, whom she bribes with banana bread to help her win at bingo."

"Yup," he said, though not sounding like he cared either way. "She pays me in banana bread too."

How much bread had my mother been making recently, and why had I not noticed?

"You know," Benji said, pursing his lips. He always did that when he was in deep thought. "Maybe your mom could talk to Carlos without him being suspicious. She could find out where he went after the town meeting the night Don died and why he's interested in our Friday night game group. It's possible he wants to keep tabs on us to keep us from getting too close to the truth."

"Then why didn't he stop by your house as well?"

Benji lifted a shoulder. "Maybe he did. Your mom said they got bored and went to the diner, remember?"

I brought two plates of huevos rancheros over to the table and set one in front of him. "You want my mother to spy for you."

Benji breathed in the smell of the green chile sauce, then glanced over at me. "More like do her civic duty."

After shoving a large bite of egg and tortilla into my mouth, I mumbled, "You know she'll do it. She can't help herself. But if Carlos ends up being our arsonist, she'll never forgive you for sending the official bingo caller to jail. Who else would agree to help her cheat in exchange for banana bread?"

13

The Pletcher home was a lot more ominous in the evening. The sun was just beginning to set, and shadows were thrown across their yard in strange ways, setting me on edge. I wondered if Angel was watching Benji and me make our way up her walkway and to the courtyard gate. Probably. Benji had called her and asked if we could stop by with some huevos rancheros.

Angel had been hesitant but ultimately agreed. Flash wasn't happy about the leftovers disappearing, but he accepted that it was for the greater good.

"Do you think your mom will come through for us?" Benji asked as we reached the gate.

His question startled me out of my thoughts. It was a good thing too. I'd been imagining Angel with her gun again. It was amazing how I could go my entire life without ever fearing someone, and then suddenly being terrified that if I said the wrong thing or looked at them the wrong way, they'd do something terrible.

"Yeah, of course. She loves meddling." I raised my hand to knock on the gate, but it swung open before I had the chance. My paranoia hadn't been completely unfounded. Angel had been watching.

She didn't say anything at first, only gestured for us to enter, and I hoped we'd made the correct decision by coming there.

"We brought you dinner," I said, hoping I sounded relaxed and happy to be there, and not like I thought she could have a mental breakdown at any moment.

To my relief, Angel smiled and opened the front door for us. "You have no idea how much I appreciate it. The last couple of days have been a blur, and I haven't had the chance to think about eating, let alone cooking." She glanced back to the tray I held. "It smells amazing. I'd forgotten how hungry I was."

Looked like the old Angel was back.

I followed her inside and set the tray on her kitchen counter. "We've already eaten. This is all yours. And I just wanted to let you know how truly sorry I am for yesterday. We should have called before visiting. I'm sure everything with Jake has been so stressful, and we only made it worse."

Angel was already shaking her head before I finished. "You are not allowed to apologize. I know I acted like I had lost my mind. After Sheriff Potts dropped in unexpectedly and took Jake away, every uninvited visitor became a threat. And to be fair, some of them were. But I should never have pulled that gun out of Jake's nightstand drawer. He keeps it there for emergencies, and even though he took a gun safety course a few years back, neither of us has touched it since. To be honest, I'm not sure I would even know how to use it if needed. Guess I should have taken the class with him. The safety on the gun was still on, and I don't know how to take it off." She winced, as if yesterday's memory still haunted her. "It's probably better that way."

"Well, we just want you to know that if you need anything, you can count on us. You just let Benji or me know what we can do."

Angel gave us a grateful smile. "The kids are still with my mom, so, unless you can get Jake out of jail, I'm not sure there is much left you can help with."

I looked to Benji for the next step. I'd said too much when we'd been at Buck's house, and I didn't want to make the same mistake.

"We'd like to try to bring him home, if it's okay with you," Benji told her, his voice soft and his eyes kind. "We know Jake didn't start that fire. He doesn't deserve the hand he's been dealt."

Angel's eyes filled with tears. "Thank you for saying that," she choked out. "But I'm not sure there's anything to be done. Sheriff Potts says she has a lighter with Jake's fingerprints on it. And there's an eyewitness, but she won't tell me who."

That was unfortunate. It looked like this might be another dead end.

"Is there anything else she told you?" Benji asked. "Even if you don't think it is relevant."

Angel shook her head. "No, nothing. In the sheriff's defense, she didn't look like she wanted to arrest Jake and she really had hoped we had some way to prove he didn't do it. Honestly, that lighter could have belonged to anyone. We sell them loose in a bin up by the cash register at the store, and Jake restocks it every evening."

My gaze snapped to Benji.

That was both wonderful and terrible at the same time. It was great because it meant that Jake and Benji's friends might not be suspects at all. But it also meant that we were further from discovering who the true arsonist was.

Benji avoided my gaze, but his lips twitched, like he was trying to restrain whatever emotion was begging to burst out. "The night of the fire, did Jake go back out after you put the twins to bed?" he asked. "Or were you both home for the night, doing your usual routine?"

Angel hesitated, and she didn't need to say anything more for me to know what it meant. Jake hadn't been home, and the problem wasn't that it was Angel's word against the eyewitness. The problem was that Jake didn't have an alibi. That was the real reason he was in jail.

I wondered if Angel was having her own doubts about Jake's innocence. Maybe she thought he'd done something in the spirit of protecting their family, and our town.

Maybe that was why she'd temporarily gone over-the-top defensive the day before.

"What time did he come back?" I asked, my voice quiet.

Angel heaved a long sigh and slumped onto a bar stool at the counter. "I don't know. Late. The twins developed a fever around midnight, and because nothing local is open that late, he had to drive forty-five minutes to the city. Jake is that kind of guy—always helping, never complaining."

"What did you tell Sheriff Potts?" Benji asked. I understood why he was asking. If Angel had lied and said Jake had been home, and the sheriff discovered it, it would only hurt Jake's case.

Angel lifted her gaze until it met Benji's. "I told her the truth. But she asked which pharmacy he had gone to, and I didn't know. Jake is always the one who runs emergency errands while I stay home with the kids."

"And he wasn't able to give her any specifics?" he asked.

"No," Angel said, her voice weak. "Sheriff Potts said Jake claims he stopped at the first place he saw, and he gave her an approximate location, but it wasn't specific enough, and she hasn't been able to corroborate his story. When she asked to see a receipt, he didn't have one. He always tells the cashier he doesn't want it—that it will end up being just another piece of trash in his car."

Everything about Jake's story was too vague to be useful, and knowing that a hundred of Jake's lighters could be floating around town, we had way too many potential suspects.

"I know you probably don't want to think about this," I started, my words slow. "But is there anyone you know who might have had a quarrel with Jake? Maybe an unsatisfied customer or—"

"Or a friend he might have had a falling out with," Angel finished. She didn't seem offended by the question. On the contrary, she looked like she'd been expecting it. "Sheriff Potts asked the same thing. Jake doesn't have an enemy in the world. He's loved by everyone. That being said..." She hesitated, and her gaze flicked to Benji before it returned to me. "Even though the sheriff wouldn't tell me who the eyewitness was, she did tell me they described the person they saw as roughly Jake's height and build. And wearing a bright pink ball cap."

A rush of air escaped me. I knew of several people who owned a similar hat. Benji and his friends had participated in a breast cancer awareness walkathon two years earlier in memory of Jake's sister, who had passed away from cancer. As part of the free swag, they'd all received bright pink baseball caps to wear as they walked. As far as I knew, Jake was the only one who wore his on a regular basis.

"Everyone in town knows if they see that pink cap, it's Jake," Angel said.

"But you've already disproved the sheriff's lighter theory. Surely this one is just as easy to disprove," I said. "Jake isn't the only one in town who owns one."

Benji bent his head and massaged his eyebrows. "Yes,

but you understand what this means. Our suspect pool is back to its original size."

Three of Jake's best friends. Three men who were more like brothers.

Cal, Buck, and Lou.

Angel looked between Benji and me. "What suspect pool?"

"It's nothing," Benji said quickly. "Just idle thoughts as we try to make sense of everything. We know Jake didn't start the fire, but narrowing it down has proven difficult."

"Don't I know it," Angel said. "I've been thinking, Lou said there were multiple points of origin, and that's a big construction site. Maybe it wasn't a one-man job."

That wasn't such a far-fetched idea, and I was suddenly overwhelmed by the magnitude of it all. There were too many who had wanted Don Mendes to leave town. Too many who'd had access to those lighters.

But only five I knew of who owned pink baseball caps, and I was dating one of them.

Was it possible that more than one of them was involved? Had the brothers banded together to bring Don Mendes's company down?

Of course, there was also the one question I didn't want to ask.

Was Jake innocent, or had he done more than pick up medicine while he'd been out that night?

14

After making sure Angel was going to be okay for the evening and promising her we'd do everything in our power to help, we left her with the huevos rancheros. She'd already started in on them before we'd made it out the door.

"That went better than I expected," Benji said, taking my hand as we walked back to the car.

Funny, I had had the opposite reaction. "How so?"

"Angel looks like she's feeling better, for starters. And that was good information she gave us."

I nodded slowly, and he gave me a questioning look.

"It was also a lot of information," I said. "I feel we know less now than before we visited Angel. For all we know, Jake really did do it. Him and his pink hat."

I sucked in a long breath and blinked back tears, the overwhelm of the situation washing over me.

"Hey, what's going on?" Benji asked, stopping mid-step. He placed a finger under my chin and tilted my face up until our eyes met. "I've been asking too much of you, haven't I?"

I began to shake my head, but then stopped, and my gaze dropped. "I've been really stressed at work, and there's been all this freak-out over real estate developers for the past few months, and now with Jake's arrest—it's a lot."

"Do I stress you out when I talk about the local issues with your mom over dinner?" Benji asked, his eyes filled with concern.

I gave a little nod.

"And when I talk about my and your future together?"

I hesitated but then gave another little nod. "I love you, Benji. You know I do. But right now I feel like I'm only able to handle one day at a time. And even that is questionable."

Benji pulled me in and kissed the top of my head. "I'm taking you home and tucking you into bed so you can get the rest you need. And I promise I won't bring up anything to do with the future of our town, or the future of us. We're officially a day-by-day couple."

"Thank you," I whispered, batting away my tears. "It won't be like this forever. But today, it's what I need." Whatever I'd done to deserve such an amazing person as Benji in my life, I was grateful. Not everyone got a second chance. "Do you think the diner is still open? Some ice cream might help, and we haven't had much of a date this week."

Benji laughed and pulled me toward the car. "I think that can be arranged."

WE CAUGHT Melinda fifteen minutes before closing. She wasn't happy about our late arrival, but because it was only ice cream we wanted, she seemed to handle it better than usual. She even agreed to give us an extra scoop of ice cream plus some toppings because we said we'd take it to go.

I loved walking through downtown Amor at night. It was beautiful, the way the lights lit up against the night. And doing it while eating ice cream and strolling with the love of my life? It was practically magic.

Or it was until we made the mistake of walking past Town Hall. The sheriff's office and holding cells were nestled in the basement, and Danielle was just exiting through the front doors.

Normally I enjoyed seeing her, but not tonight. Not in my peaceful Benji moment. Not with Jake still sitting in his cell, and me wondering if he belonged there.

"Maddie and Benji," Danielle said, sounding surprised. "What are you two doing here? Not trying to get in and talk to Jake, I hope. I've wasted an entire day explaining to people why they can't see him. Everyone has an excuse, though. Between that and Bob insisting I make his missing gavel a priority—yes, even above a murder investigation— I'm afraid my patience has worn thin."

Benji took my free hand and squeezed it, letting me know he'd handle the situation. His hand was sticky, and normally that would make me squirm, but right now I was grateful for sticky ice cream and a boyfriend who so readily showed affection.

"Just out for date night," Benji said, holding up his half-eaten ice cream cone. Mine was melting so fast, the ice cream was practically cascading down the sides of the cone at this point, and I was using my tongue to try to catch the drips before they reached my hand. It was a losing battle.

The sheriff's lips quirked up at the edges. "I see." Her eyes took in Main Street. Most of the windows were darkened, but the exterior lights and streetlamps were still on. Her gaze then moved up to the sky, where all the stars had begun to gather. "It's a perfect night for it. I can't remember the last time I bought ice cream."

"Maybe you can convince Melinda to open back up for you. Tell her you need to do a surprise inspection of the ice cream machine, and that, while she's at it, maybe she should make you a cone. Just to make sure it's not tainted."

Danielle laughed. "I may be sheriff, but my courage has its limits. Besides, I don't want to trouble Melinda. I hear she's preparing for her CPA exam, and I don't want to be the cause of her not fulfilling a lifelong dream of becoming an accountant."

It was still difficult to believe that Melinda would soon be helping people prepare their taxes—and by choice—but that went to show you couldn't judge a cranky diner owner by her cover.

I hesitated, a question gnawing at me. "We took some dinner over to Angel tonight. I know Jake isn't allowed visitors, but has she at least been able to see him?"

Danielle's gaze settled on me, and she stayed quiet for longer than made me comfortable. "Because you two seem to be friends, and you care about Angel as such, I will say I'm worried about her. I told her she can come to see Jake as often as she likes, but the visits need to be supervised. She came by only once and hasn't returned since. She's also refusing my phone calls."

"You did arrest her husband, so I don't find that too surprising. I mean, I know you were just doing your job, but I'm sure she doesn't see it that way."

Danielle groaned. "I didn't want to arrest Jake. I like the guy, even if his children terrify me. But my job is to discover who committed a crime, arrest them, and ensure justice is served. Wherever that may lead me. And in this case, it has led me to Jake."

Benji tilted his head, his eyes scrutinizing. "But you know the lighter you found is sold in his hardware store, right? He has a whole bin of loose lighters, and Jake is the one who restocks them. You could find his fingerprints on about two-hundred lighters on any given day."

Sheriff Potts stilled. "I...did know that. But that doesn't mean he is off the hook."

I'd been so distracted by the sheriff that I'd completely forgotten about my ice cream. I looked down and discovered that, thanks to New Mexico's warm evenings, the ice cream was nothing more than a liquid mess dripping down my arm and onto my shoes.

I glanced around but didn't see a trash can, so now I was stuck holding a sticky, soggy cone and wouldn't be able to clean up until I got home.

"It doesn't make sense," I said, holding the cone away from my body to mitigate the damage. "Everyone had motive to get rid of Don Mendes, and plenty of people had access to one of Jake's lighters. We'd originally thought it was one of the people closest to Jake's family, but really, it could be anyone."

The sheriff held up a finger. "Hold on. Why did you think it was one of the people closest to him? Have you been investigating this case?"

"Of course not," I said, heat rushing into my cheeks, knowing I'd just blown it. I gave Danielle my most innocent of faces. "It was just a passing thought. I mean, why else would someone frame him if they didn't have a close connection?"

"And now you think he was purposely framed."

Danielle shook her head. "Okay, you two. What have you discovered?"

I shared a look with Benji, wondering how much we were willing to share.

He turned to the sheriff. "We'd like to speak with Jake. Just to see how he's doing and pass along any messages he has for Angel."

"I knew it. You are investigating," she said. "After you promised me you weren't going to interfere."

"We didn't mean to, honest," I said.

The sheriff raised an eyebrow, her lips pulling up at the corners. "You've accidentally been investigating this case?"

I nodded. "Yup. Cross my heart, hope to die." I crossed my heart with my finger like I used to do as a kid, but then winced. The childhood saying I had done with my friends didn't work as well in this setting. Not in reference to a murder investigation.

"It isn't Maddie's fault," Benji said, resting his hand on the small of my back. "I dragged her into this. Jake is my friend, and his family needs him. You have reasonable doubt, and I wanted to make sure you had as much of it as possible. Trust me when I say that we can help you."

Danielle's eyes narrowed in suspicion. "How so?"

"Right now we are the only ones Angel trusts."

Danielle shook her head. "That doesn't matter. She's told me all she's going to. Angel has no idea where Jake was that night or who he might have been with. I don't need her help."

She had a point. We needed more clues. Something that would at least point us in the right direction.

"Please," I said. "I know you aren't convinced Jake burned down the construction site, but you also can't place an entire town under suspicion of murder—an entire town who happens to have motive. Let us talk to Jake. Maybe something he tells us will be of some use."

I wasn't sure I had convinced her, but Danielle ultimately raised her hands in defeat. "Fine. Since Jake's initial arrest, he's refused to speak to me. It has something to do with me telling him anything he said could be used against him in a court of law. Maybe you can do better." She turned and pointed a finger at me. "But if you hold back information—"

I laughed. "We both know you are going to be listening through your security cameras that you no doubt have all over that place." The sheriff's movements stilled, and her lips tightened. I tilted my head, studying her. "Your security cameras are down."

"Not the visuals," she quickly said. "Just the sound."

"That's why your visit with Angel was supervised. And why she hasn't returned to see him."

"It's been down for five months now, and I'm annoyed that repairing it isn't high on anyone's priority list. Buck was supposed to come out last week, but at the last minute he said something came up. He told me the same thing this week. Maybe next week he'll surprise me by coming out, but I'm doubtful."

Yet Buck had had time to rig the outlets in Don's hotel room.

"We'll tell you everything Jake says," I promised her. And I intended to keep that promise.

Unless there was a good reason I couldn't.

I'd treat it as a case-by-case basis.

15

I'd never actually been down to the sheriff's office before, a fact I was proud of, and I hadn't known what to expect. I tossed the remnants of my ice cream cone into a nearby garbage can and then Benji and I followed the sheriff into the elevator on Town Hall's main floor. As we descended, it was slow and squeaky and it prolonged the experience, making me feel like we were being led to a dungeon.

That was the first time I wanted to turn around.

The second was when we stepped out. The fluorescent lights on the basement level were blinding, and I had to cover my eyes until the spots disappeared.

As they did so, I slowly lowered my hand, and my gaze swept over the open space. It was one giant room, nothing hidden. The two holding cells were on the opposite end of the room, while the sheriff's and deputy's desks sat next to us. Filing cabinets, printers, and a small table with chairs sat in the middle of the room.

From the looks of it, every visit would be supervised, with or without the cameras.

"I know it doesn't look like much," Danielle said. "But it's home."

"It's cozy," I said. "Of course, you have zero privacy. Those you arrest no doubt can hear every word exchanged between you and your deputy."

"The acoustics are actually quite terrible." Danielle motioned for us to follow her. "I can be sitting at my desk and not hear a word that is being said on the other side of the room. Hence, we still need audio on the security cameras. It's like the sheriff's station was an afterthought when they built your town."

It probably had been. I didn't know the history of my town, but I did know that if you were a criminal and needed to get out of Amor fast, there was literally only one road you could take to leave. Not only that, but we were nestled between four towns that were forty-five minutes in each direction. If you committed a major crime, there was nowhere to run. The cops from any of those towns would be on you before you figured out where you even were.

"That's not surprising," I said, already getting a headache from the fluorescent lights. "You should talk to town council about at least getting you a decent office. I can't believe this is where you have to come to work every day. If I were one of your prisoners, I'd confess just so I could get out of here."

Danielle's lips pulled down into a frown. "Gee, thanks."

Benji gave me a warning look. We still hadn't gotten what we'd come for—a conversation with Jake—and I was insulting the sheriff's workplace.

"And by that," I said slowly, "I meant, I love what you've done with the place."

Danielle looked like she was fighting a smile, but it broke through. "It's all right. I promised you a conversation with Jake, and I'll keep that promise. But if he says anything that could help close this case—"

"You'll be the first to know." I used my finger to cross my heart but left out the words this time. She got the gist.

Benji and I turned toward the two holding cells. At first I didn't see Jake, and I hoped he hadn't made a run for it. A couple of years earlier, the sheriff's former deputy had jimmied the locks, allowing two prisoners to escape. Of course, Danielle had gotten a new deputy and two new locks since then. These ones were electronic. Fancy.

As we walked toward the cells, butterflies erupted in my stomach. Not because I thought Jake had escaped but because I didn't know what I was going to say to him. This was a man I'd seen every week, sometimes every day, as I walked to my therapy office. He always smiled and said hello, and asked how Flash and Lilly were doing.

Now he was locked up, and I was going to be the one asking the questions. But they weren't going to be about the twins or Angel or the new employee who was always making a mess of things at his shop. These would be questions about who might have a grudge against Jake, if he had been anywhere near the construction site the night of the fire, and who he thought might have killed Don Mendes.

I had a reputation in town for involving myself in murder investigations. Jake would know why I was here. And our previous interactions would mean nothing.

"Hey, Jake," Benji said, approaching the holding cells.

I stepped to Benji's side and saw that Jake was lying on a small cot in the far corner. No wonder I hadn't been able to see him. The prisoners probably placed it there to get whatever privacy they could.

Jake stirred and pushed himself up into a sitting position, blinking against the harsh light. He had only been in there a couple of days now, but stubble was growing on his chin. A to-go box from the diner was stashed under the cot, so at least they were feeding him decent food.

Jake started to stand, but Benji waved a hand at him. "Don't get up on account of us."

The hardware store owner paused, as if trying to decide what to do, but ultimately got to his feet and lumbered over to us. "Needed to stretch anyhow."

Benji nodded, like he'd expected as much. "How's the new guy working out at the store? He still stocking PVC pipes in the power tool aisle?"

Jake chuckled. "I think I got him straightened out. He's a good kid and is getting used to the layout."

I had been wrong. Turned out we were asking about the trivial stuff. "The twins are getting big," I said. "They'll be climbing the counters before you know it."

Both Jake and Benji started, like they'd forgotten I was there, and neither looked like the interruption had been welcome.

Maybe there was an unspoken way this conversation was supposed to go, and I hadn't been clued in.

I fell silent as Jake released a long sigh. "Yes, they will. I only hope I'll be around to see it."

Oh. Right.

I was usually in my element in these kinds of situations —talking people through hard times and helping them open up. By the ends of my sessions with patients, they would thank me for helping them see the world in a way they'd never allowed themselves to.

I had a feeling this was not one of those sessions, and I wondered if it would be better if I excused myself and let Benji take the reins on this one. He'd been a lot better at this than me as of late, and I was worried I'd only make things worse.

Jake looked to Benji. "I'm surprised our sheriff allowed you in here at all. She's been keeping everyone else away, including Angel."

Benji gave Jake a kind smile. "Danielle is a good woman just trying to do her job, and she hasn't been keeping Angel away. Your wife can come any time she likes."

"Sure, but Sheriff Potts will be listening in on every word. The visits have to be supervised."

Benji raised a shoulder, conceding Jake's point. "Guess the only thing to do about it is to get you out of here."

I expected Jake to perk up—to get excited at the thought. I'd expected...hope.

Instead, Jake's entire countenance fell further. "How do you expect that to happen, huh? Someone wearing my hat was seen near the site. They have my fingerprints. And it was no secret I wouldn't sell my shop to Don. He'd been by that morning for the fifteenth time, trying to get me to sell, and I threatened him. Told him not to come back."

I wouldn't be telling the sheriff that last part. People gave empty threats all the time to try to convey the seriousness of a message. It didn't mean anything. Of course, the recipient of those empty threats didn't usually show up dead.

Benji nodded slowly. "If he was such a problem, why weren't you at the town meeting that night?"

Jake snort-laughed. "And give that man any more of my time and attention? No way. He'd already stolen enough of that from me. My family goes on walks every evening, and that night wasn't going to be any different."

I leaned against the bars on the adjacent cell. Jake certainly didn't sound like someone who'd had the intention of visiting a construction site and burning the place down. But that wasn't going to convince anyone else of his innocence.

"And then what?" Benji continued. "You went home, around midnight the twins developed a fever, and you left to get medicine."

Jake nodded. "Yeah. That is one of the things I'm grateful for with all this new development—that emergency clinic and pharmacy they're building on the corner of Main and Las Colinas." He paused, as if gathering his thoughts. "It's not development I'm against. If this Don Mendes situation scares everyone off, we lose the benefits we've been waiting a long time for. But I don't take kindly to being forced out of my own store."

"Of course not," Benji said. "But if someone were to give you a fair price and a good contract, would you be willing to sell to them?"

Jake hesitated, his gaze bouncing between Benji and me, as if he were trying to determine if we could be trusted. Ultimately, he decided to take the gamble. "I would consider it. But it would have to be in my favor and allow me to open my store in a better location. I'm not going to sell if I'm not coming out ahead."

He almost sounded like he was afraid to admit that he was okay with development. Like there would be repercussions if anyone found out.

We were all quiet for a moment, each lost in our own thoughts. Or at least I was. Benji and Jake seemed to be able to understand what the other was thinking, no verbal communication required. And I was a bit envious. Even with Trish, I'd never had that, and we lived together.

What was it Benji and Jake weren't saying?

"You're thinking it was Carlos," Benji finally said.

I tried to hide my shock at Benji's bluntness. Why was it that I couldn't get away with stuff like that? I already knew the answer. Benji was one of the gang. He was an insider. And it made me wonder why he'd wanted me here in the first place.

Jake nodded slowly. "The thought crossed my mind. He's changed since being elected to town council, and we haven't exactly seen eye to eye."

"I heard he found out you didn't vote for him."

Another nod. "Yup. For some reason, he had this idea I'd be voting for him because he shops at my store, but everyone in town does. It's purely business. What he does with his outdoor rec store on his own time doesn't affect me whatsoever. What he does on town council absolutely does. Don't know why it matters; he won anyway."

"Did Carlos say something to you?"

"No, but Bob gave me a heads up. I've noticed there's been something accusatory in the way Carlos has looked at me ever since. I guess he thought we were closer than we are."

"What about Cal or Buck?"

Jake scratched the back of his neck, and his gaze dropped. The question clearly made him uncomfortable.

Was it because he suspected either of them could have done it, but he didn't want to think about the possibility?

"Neither have good things to say about Don Mendes," he finally said.

But that wasn't the real question here. This was no longer about who had started the fire and inadvertently killed Don. This was about who had betrayed Jake. Who would be willing to tear his family apart.

And who had gotten away with it.

'

16

B enji rested his head against the bars, as if this line of questioning had taken far more out of him than he'd anticipated.

"If you tell me you had nothing to do with this, I'll believe you," he said softly. "I'll place your word above anyone else. I won't shy away from the hard questions. But you have to tell me if you went anywhere near that construction site."

Jake shook his head. "I swear, I didn't. My pink baseball cap is right where it always is, on a hook by the door. I was in such a rush to get the medicine that I forgot to grab it."

"Pharmacies all have security cameras," Benji said. "The sheriff can't find you on any of them."

Jake looked at him in surprise. "That's because it wasn't a pharmacy. At least, I don't think it was. It was late, and the usual one I go to was closed. I had to find one of those twenty-four-hour stores that had some generic medicine on the shelves. I don't know the name of it, but I told the sheriff it was right off the first or second exit."

Somehow the sheriff had misinterpreted that information.

"You think they have security cameras?" Benji asked.

"Definitely. That place was super sketchy. I made sure to get in and out as quickly as possible—it wasn't the type of place you want to stick around late at night. But even if she finds me on the footage, it won't matter."

Benji tilted his head. "That would prove your innocence and force the sheriff to look elsewhere."

Jake released a defeated sigh. "Lou knows where the fire started, but he has no idea *when* it started. The place was pretty much gone by the time he showed up. The only thing he did was spray everything down and make sure all the embers were out. It could have been started at any time, and I didn't get home until after two a.m."

"Proving your innocence is no longer enough. We need to find who did it," I said. Both heads swiveled toward me, and I realized I had meant to stay quiet.

Jake's gaze bored into me, and I had to use all my self-control not to wither under it. "That's easier said than done," he finally said. "If someone really did set me up to take the fall, you'd need evidence they were even there, let alone starting fires. How do you intend to do that?"

That was a very good question.

"First I'd lay out all potential suspects so I could look at them equally," I said. "Sometimes it's the quiet ones who surprise you."

Looking at the two men in front of me, I knew this tactic was never going to work. Jake was too close to the situation. As was Benji. Neither of them would be able to look at their friends with a critical eye, even if they thought they were guilty, and I didn't blame them. I wouldn't want to either. That was why people like Sheriff Potts existed— someone who was paid to only look at the evidence.

"Why don't I leave you two to ponder what you'd like to do," I said, stepping away and then rejoining Danielle at her desk.

"Anything?" she asked.

I shook my head. "I'm certain Jake didn't do it, but that's all I'm sure of. He's right about one thing. Even if you find him on the security cameras at whatever twenty-four-hour convenience store he visited, it won't be enough to prove his innocence."

Only Jake, Benji, and their friends had the pink ball caps. They had driven two hours to go to that walkathon in memory of Jake's sister. It wasn't like it had been a town event.

Danielle was watching me closely. She knew I was holding back. "Who is in this Friday night group that they don't want to consider? That's what you're thinking, isn't it —that one of their friends set Jake up?"

I stared, and she laughed.

"Please, give me some credit for being good at my job.

Those guys have been playing cards every Friday night for as long as I've lived in Amor," she said. "I know about the pink hats, and I know that it takes some planning to pin a crime on another person. You generally need to know them well. Be close to them. And this Friday night group is the closest Jake has to that. So, who do they not want to talk about?"

Of course she wanted names.

I was saved from answering when my phone rang. I pulled it from my purse with two fingers as I tried to avoid spreading melted ice cream, though my fingers still stuck to the phone as I did so. My mom's picture was displayed on the screen.

She might have information on Carlos. I hadn't ruled him out yet.

It would be suspicious if I didn't answer it, but there was nowhere I could go to get some privacy. Maybe there was a bathroom.

Danielle raised an eyebrow. "You going to get that?"

"It's my mom, so yes, I suppose I should." I gave what I hoped was an easy laugh. "I'll be just a minute." I touched the green phone icon as I stood, my gaze sweeping the room. There was one door that could lead to the bathrooms, but it had an electronic keypad next to it.

At least this place had terrible acoustics.

"Hey, Mom. How's bingo going?" I moved to the table in the center of the room, where Danielle shouldn't be able to hear, based on what she'd told Benji and me when we'd first arrived.

"Great. I won a Pilates DVD. So, I guess I'm one of those people now." My mom sounded grumpy that she'd had no say in the matter. "Tell me, do you need to own yoga pants to do Pilates? If so, I'm going to have to go to the mall to buy some, and I'm not in the mood to drive two hours just so I can pretend that I'm going to take up exercise."

"You could always order a pair online."

My mom snorted. "Yeah, and risk having my identity stolen. I don't think so."

"Or you could choose to not do Pilates and give the DVD away like you did with your Harry Potter winnings."

A pause. "I feel bad winning and then giving away the prizes, but they don't tell you what the prize is before you play."

"You mean, you feel bad because you cheat?"

My mom immediately jumped to her own defense. "Who told you that? I bet it was Flash, wasn't it, that little tattletale."

"Hold on, that's your grandson you're talking about. And you're the one bribing him."

A long sigh. "I suppose you're right." A pause. "Do you think Flash would enjoy Pilates? That boy is stiff as a board from sitting in his computer chair all day long. It would probably do him some good."

I stifled a laugh. The thought of Flash doing Pilates was

hilarious, and I kind of wanted to see it. "Definitely," I said. "But is that really why you're calling? To tell me you cheated some old ladies out of a Pilates DVD?" I lowered my voice. Danielle had said she couldn't hear a thing from the other end of the room, but I didn't want to take any chances. "What about Carlos? You said you were going to talk to him."

"Patience. I was getting to it." My mom then fell silent, and I wondered if the call had dropped. I glanced at the screen and saw it was still connected.

"Mom?"

"Sorry, I got distracted. I'm just about to leave, but one of the ladies is demanding to see the bingo balls up at the front table. I think she's catching on. Looks like I need to lie low for the next couple of weeks."

I rubbed my eyebrows. "Mom, focus. Was Carlos willing to talk to you?"

"Of course he was. I have a sweet and innocent aura about me. It wasn't a matter of getting him to talk, it was a matter of getting him to stop."

Said the woman who was cheating at bingo.

"Okay. So...what did he say?"

My mom harrumphed. "I was getting to that part. He said that after the town meeting, he went on a long walk to calm down. He did pass the construction site, but it was standing and in good form. Got home around ten o'clock and went to bed. He did say he wouldn't be surprised if one of the elderly residents in town was the arsonist because as he was walking, half the town stopped him to thank him for his service, and most of them attend bingo night."

"I highly doubt that someone went off-roading with their walker to set the construction site on fire," I said, though I kind of loved the idea of it. "He's just saying that so it takes some of the heat off of him. Even if he didn't set the fire himself and kill Don, it's because of Carlos that it burned down in the first place. He's the one telling everyone we need to take drastic measures, and he had to have known how dangerous spreading fear is."

"I guess, but according to him, he hadn't meant to get the town riled up, he just wanted everyone to see the danger of allowing these developers to infiltrate our town."

He had a funny way of doing it.

I glanced back toward where Danielle was at her desk, watching me, and she wasn't bothering to hide it. I hoped the acoustics in here were as bad as she claimed they were. My gaze shifted to Benji and Jake, who were much closer to me. Their heads were together, and they were deep in conversation. Even though they likely could have heard me if they wanted to, they didn't even glance my way.

"So, what do you think, Mom? Could Carlos have had something to do with the fire and Don's death?"

She hesitated and seemed to be choosing her words carefully, which wasn't something she often did. She was more of a shoot-from-the-hip kind of communicator.

"I did ask if he thought the person who'd set the fire

had gone too far, and he didn't have a good answer for me. He felt the incident had been tragic, but he also said that sometimes fire needed to be fought with fire. The analogy in this case is a bit too literal for my liking, but there you have it."

"Do you think he did it?" I asked again. She was skirting the issue, and I believed it was on purpose.

"Carlos is a passionate man," my mom said, her words slow. "And I don't think he's completely off the mark with his views on town development. But did he start that fire and kill Don Mendes, then allow Jake to take the fall for it? No. I don't believe he did."

I knew I had asked my mom to talk to Carlos for me, but I wondered if she'd been the right one for the job. She was sympathetic to his cause, and in spite of her some-times aggressive personality, she usually tried to see the good in people.

"How firm are you in that belief?" I asked. "I know he's your bingo cheating partner and everything, but—"

"Maddie, you asked for my help, and you need to trust me for once," she interrupted. "One of the reasons it was so difficult for me to get Carlos to stop talking was because he kept asking about Jake. It was annoying, really. He said that ever since Angel ran him off the day of Jake's arrest, he hasn't been allowed near their place. He's worried about them, and yet he knows they think he likely did it. That they think he's the natural choice to have killed a guy and thrown Jake to the wolves. AKA, Sheriff Potts." She paused.

"Carlos didn't have many friends growing up, but I'm sure you already know that. Despite everyone going to high school together, and let's be honest, there were only forty kids in your graduating class, Carlos was always one of the quiet ones who hung back. It wasn't until recently that he finally broke out of his shell."

Okay, so the man had quietly been in the background and was slow to make friends for most of his life. My heart went out to the guy. But many criminals had similar stories.

"That doesn't prove his innocence," I said.

My mom released a long sigh. "No, but why do you think he's so outspoken now? Because people are finally listening. At least they were. Until this unfortunate incident. And that's all he wanted. To be seen. You're someone who has always tried to help those who needed it most—that's why you went into psychology, isn't it? Doesn't Carlos deserve someone who believes in him? Who doesn't automatically assume him guilty because he wasn't part of the in-group?"

She was right. In high school, Carlos had been one of those people who kind of just blended in with the surroundings. I couldn't tell you if he'd attended any of the dances, or even graduation. He had just been...there. Like a picture on the wall that you stop seeing because you've passed it so many times.

"Okay. I'll keep an open mind," I said. Even saying that, I felt a knot in my stomach. I didn't want it to be Cal or

Buck or Lou. But I couldn't let this turn into a popularity contest. The in-group meant nothing anymore. It didn't matter how much I liked them.

Someone was willing to let Jake go to prison for them. And I had to make sure that never happened.

17

When I returned to the sheriff's desk, she watched me above steepled fingers. "Everything okay?"

I gave a little nod and settled back into the seat across from her. I wished Benji would hurry. "Yeah, she's at bingo night and won a Pilates DVD. It's already doing its job because she's feeling guilty about not exercising enough and she's trying to give it away before she ends up driving two hours to buy yoga pants. You interested in Pilates?"

Danielle laughed, though it was guarded. "Thanks, but I think I'm good."

"Yeah, me too."

She looked like she wanted to push more about the phone call but U-turned back to the topic at hand. The very thing I'd been trying to avoid.

"Do you think anyone in Jake and Benji's Friday night group is capable of doing something like this? Anyone that would be willing to let Jake take the fall for something they did?"

Danielle was more blunt than usual. Which meant she thought she was close to cracking the case wide open. And I now realized the only reason she'd allowed Benji and me down to see Jake was because of this moment. She wasn't interested in what Jake had to say. She was interested in what we already knew.

When I didn't say anything, Danielle leaned back in her chair. "Cal, Buck, and Lou have all been a part of the Friday night gang since the beginning. Jake is not going to want to suspect them. That leaves Carlos high on his list of potential suspects, considering his recent stint in politics, and how vocal he is." She paused. "Benji has a pink ball cap, does he not?"

I jumped from my chair. "Oh no you don't. There is no way Benji is involved."

"It's not even a possibility?"

No, it wasn't. Because I knew Benji. I loved him. And he wasn't capable of what she was suggesting.

Danielle's gaze never wavered as she studied me. She was better at reading people than most gave her credit for, and it was unnerving.

"Do you think Cal or Lou are any more likely?" she asked after an uncomfortable moment.

I squeezed my eyes shut, not wanting to answer this question either. Because I couldn't see Cal or Lou lighting a building on fire, let alone killing a guy—accidental or not.

Like Benji and Jake, I was biased, and I wasn't going to apologize for it.

"Maybe it wasn't any of them," I said, my voice weak. Because if it hadn't been one of them wearing that baseball cap, who had it been?

"Maybe. I am following other leads. But in the meantime, wouldn't you say that those five are our best bet? If you are confident that Jake is innocent."

Five. Not four. Which meant she was including Benji in her list of suspects. All because of that stupid walkathon hat.

And Danielle had said *we*, as if she was now including me in her investigation. Because of my proximity to Benji and his friends.

I had a feeling I knew where she was going with this.

She wanted me to spy.

But I wouldn't do it. And I told her as much.

"I understand," she said. "But there is something you should know." Danielle paused, her eyes looking sad. "I heard back from Dr. Harris today. Not all of Don's injuries were from the burning beams falling on him. He'd been hit in the back of the head before the fire even started."

I paused. "You mean, someone killed him, then started the fire to cover their tracks."

Danielle raised a shoulder. "Looks like it. Regardless, I

have twenty-four hours before I need to officially charge Jake with murder." She hesitated. "I can't let him go, Maddie. Not without good cause. Not with the evidence I have."

This was no longer an arson case with involuntary manslaughter. It was murder. And we had less than a day before Jake's future was out of our hands.

I sat on the curb in front of Town Hall, my arms resting on my knees. Moisture sprang to my eyes, and I wiped the tears away before remembering my sticky hands. I'd still not had the chance to wash them. Now, melted cream and sugar covered my face. Just what I needed on a night like this.

"You okay?"

Startled, I jumped and spun toward the voice, but it was only Edna on one of her evening walks. She wore a bright orange and green track suit with a matching orange hat.

Edna had never asked if I was okay before. Even now, I wondered if she was only asking because she wanted to be the first with the latest gossip. Maybe she thought my relationship with Benji was in trouble. She was Amor's version of a tabloid magazine, and she liked to make sure each new edition was available first thing in the morning.

"Everything's fine, but thank you," I said, straightening and forcing a smile. I was sure she could see straight through it, but she couldn't very well put *Maddie Swallows fakes smile* in tomorrow's edition of Edna's Daily Gossip. Then again, maybe she would, if it was a slow news day.

"I'd think you of all people wouldn't have anything to be upset about," Edna said with a frown. "You have a handsome boyfriend, two lovely children, and the developers won't be building in Amor after all. You have every reason to be happy."

All self-pity immediately vanished, and I stared. "What did you say?"

"Life is good," Edna said, this time with a bit of impatience. "You have a handsome—"

"No, not that part," I interrupted. "About the developers. What do you mean they aren't building here? Do you mean that Don Mendes's company is pulling out of Amor?"

"Well, sure. Didn't you hear? All the developers are pulling out. If we're going to resort to burning down their buildings and murdering their developers, and the sheriff and mayor are going to stand by and let it happen, you would too, wouldn't you?"

"But they aren't standing by," I spluttered. "It's only been two days, and Danielle is working hard to catch the arsonist. She already has Jake in custody. What more do they want?"

Edna laughed, like she was in on a joke that I hadn't been aware of. "It's not enough. They want assurances it won't happen again. Sheriff Potts and the mayor can't make those kinds of promises, so the developers are pulling out. They don't want an angry mob burning down their projects every time they begin building."

I released an exasperated sigh. "It's not like we have a gang of arsonists in Amor. This is the first time something like this has happened in the history of our town, or at least in my lifetime."

Edna didn't seem to care one way or the other and merely shrugged. "I'm just telling you how I heard it. The people have won, and Amor will stay the same as it always has—the way it was meant to be."

"But what about the emergency medical clinic and the pharmacy? Things we need. We can't attract good doctors to a dying town."

Edna placed her hands on her tiny hips, and her eyes narrowed. Now I'd done it. I'd kicked the hornet's nest, and Edna looked like she was in the mood to sting. Whether it was tonight or tomorrow morning in her tabloid gossip, she'd make sure I knew she was unhappy with me.

"Why is it that you are the only one in this town who is intent on destroying it?" she asked, taking a step toward me. She may have been short in stature, only coming up to my chest, but what she lacked in height she made up for in firepower. "You claim to be a proud member of our town, and yet you want to change everything about Amor, to the point where it will be unrecognizable."

I tried to stand my ground, but it was difficult when her gaze made me feel so small. "It's because I love Amor that I want it to thrive. And more development will only bring out the best parts. I'm not saying that Cal or Buck or Debbie should sell their shops. There are other places in town that can support the kind of development that would be healthy for Amor. Wouldn't you like to have a medical clinic you can go to twenty-four hours a day, or would you rather hope a heart attack doesn't kill you before you manage to get to the hospital?"

"That was only one time," Edna said, frowning. "And I don't plan on having another."

I didn't doubt it. She spent most of the day walking and ate mostly fresh fruits and vegetables, rarely eating meat. For fun, she spent her free time creating large ceramic frogs meant for lawn decor and sold them at the farmer's market each Saturday. She'd probably outlive the entire town at this rate.

I had never taken Edna's gossip seriously, but as she turned away to continue her walk, I thought about what she'd said about the developers pulling out of Amor, and I realized this was one time she might have gotten it right.

18

When Benji finally emerged from Town Hall, Edna was long gone and blaming me for her drop in heart rate. Apparently, she'd stopped long enough that she was no longer in her cardio zone.

"I noticed you left pretty quick," he said, walking out and shoving his hands in his pockets. "Something come up?"

I hesitated, thinking of the sheriff and what she'd told me. "I didn't know what help I'd be," I said. "You and Jake aren't exactly unbiased when it comes to creating a suspect list, and I didn't want to be the bad guy."

More like I didn't want to tell Benji that one of his friends had likely killed Don before setting the fire. It was easier to think of one of them as an arsonist than a murderer.

Benji gave a small nod. "I noticed you had a little chat with the sheriff before leaving."

"I didn't tell her anything, if that's what you're worried about."

"I wasn't."

Silence.

And then we both spoke simultaneously.

"I think Jake did it."

"You're on the sheriff's suspect list."

"What?" we both said at the same time.

I released a sigh. "Danielle is looking at other angles, but she believes the baseball cap is the proof that the arsonist is someone in your friend group, and she won't discount you. In fact, because I know you and your friends better than most, she wants me to keep an eye on all of you."

He gave a small nod. "I see."

"Which I won't, of course." I said quickly. "Then again, it's a moot point if Jake really is guilty. Which he's not. Right?"

Benji winced, like just the thought of it was painful. "I don't want him to be. But isn't it convenient that he had to drive out of town on the night the fire started and that he can't remember the name of the store he went to? Maybe it was a pharmacy, maybe it wasn't. And he thinks it's the first exit, but he's not sure. His story is literally unprovable. But it's not disprovable, either."

I rested a hand on Benji's arm. "It wasn't Jake. He and

Angel are going to be fine. And there's always the possibility that none of your friends did it. But we have to make sure." I hesitated. "Don was murdered, Benji."

He raised an eyebrow quizzically. "I know."

"No, I mean, he was murdered. Before the fire."

I watched a myriad of emotions cross Benji's face as he attempted to wrap his head around what I was telling him.

"So, when you say my friends and I are on the sheriff's suspect list, you mean she thinks one of us murdered Don and then started the fire."

My gaze dropped. "We only have twenty-four hours until she officially charges Jake. And we can't let her do that. I think we need to go around and talk to your friends. One on one."

I expected Benji to protest, but instead he slowly said, "So that instead of one friend going to prison for the next few decades, it will be one of the others. That doesn't seem a very fair trade."

"It isn't about what's fair. It's about what's right."

He gave a slight nod. "That's true. And it's also true when you say I'm too close to this. I think I should let you go ahead and see what you can find out."

"Your friends won't talk to me. Not unless you're there. Even then, they might not."

Benji blew out a hard breath and ran his fingers through his hair. "I can't wait for all this to be over. I hate every part of it." He shook out his arms and jumped side to side, as if he were preparing to enter a boxing ring. A moment passed before he calmed and turned to me. "All right. We'll see what everyone knows. We can stop by Buck and Cal's shops first thing tomorrow morning. I think it would be better visiting them there rather than at home. Then it can seem like we were just walking by. They're the only ones open on Sunday."

I nodded. "We'll start with Buck, then."

There was no way they'd think we were just in the neighborhood. Not with the kinds of questions we needed to ask. But who knew, maybe that was a good thing. Maybe we needed to make them nervous.

THE NEXT MORNING, I had one foot out the door when Flash appeared at my side, his eyes narrowed in suspicion.

"Where are you going so early? You're usually not out of your pajamas before ten o'clock on Sundays."

My ever-observant children. "I need to grab something from Buck's shop. I shouldn't be gone long."

Flash's face lit up. "Ooh, that's perfect. I have a computer I need him to look at for me. It's been running slow, and my programs keep shutting down. I'm probably just overworking it and need to upgrade it with more memory. I'd do it myself, but I just don't have the time. Which reminds me, I have a competition starting in twenty minutes. I guess I'll have to use my other computer for that." He ran back upstairs, taking the steps two at a time.

Oh, the life of a mother who had a soon-to-be professional hacker as a son. "Where is the competition based out of this time?" I called after him.

"Madrid."

Of course it was.

But unbeknown to him, Flash had just provided the perfect reason to go to Buck's. Maybe Benji and I would be able to pull this off after all.

Flash reappeared carrying a large box. "Be careful with it. I need it back in better condition than when it left the house."

So, what he was saying was *Don't drop it.*

Looked like my morning walk was going to be a morning drive instead, because there was no way I was lugging that thing all over downtown Amor.

"It will be better than new," I promised him.

Flash scrunched up his nose, like he wasn't sure if he could trust me, and then decided to put the computer in the car himself. Just in case.

As he did so, Edna was returning home from her morning walk. "Morning," she said, walking up her driveway.

"Morning," I called back. "It's a beautiful Sunday." I needed to keep the conversation on weather. Anything else was just asking for trouble.

Edna nodded. "Just how the good Lord intended it. You going to church this afternoon?"

She asked me the same question every Sunday, but we

had yet to go. It was more of a formality at this point. Not that I had anything against church, it just wasn't our thing. I preferred to stay home with the kids, since we didn't see much of each other during the week. Our tradition was a Sunday afternoon family board game session with pizza for dinner. It wasn't much, but it was something we all looked forward to.

"Not today. Maybe next week."

Edna nodded, like she believed me, then disappeared inside in a flash of bright yellow and pink. It matched the paint that was still splattered all over her driveway.

By the time I reached Buck's electronics shop, Benji was already out front waiting for me.

"Too far of a walk?" he asked, his lips tilting up, teasing me. Considering it was only a five-minute walk, he had every right.

"Flash has a computer he needs Buck to add memory to," I said, popping the trunk.

Benji's lips parted in surprise, and he nodded. "That's perfect for our purposes today."

"That's what I was thinking."

But then a sad look crossed Benji's face, and he frowned. I gave him a kiss on the cheek and held his gaze. "You don't have to go in there. None of this is fair, and I don't mind going in by myself. I have an excuse now."

Benji hesitated, and for a moment I thought he might have changed his mind, but then his eyes steeled with determination.

"We're merely going in to get Flash's computer fixed. No harm in that." What he didn't say, but his expression did, was that one of his friends may have been responsible for the death of a man, and to help save one friend and their family, he might have to betray another. That was a responsibility he'd determined to take upon himself, and he wasn't going to back out now. Benji had always been a peacekeeper, hating when people fought.

In a way, he was still doing that.

Benji lifted the computer out of the trunk and carried it for me while I locked the car.

I hated what we were about to do because I'd always liked Buck. He was fun and charismatic, the type of guy you couldn't help but like. The only reason he'd not settled down with a wife was because he had too many options and he couldn't settle on which woman he liked best. And for whatever reason, the women stuck around, knowing they had competition but hoping that in the end he would choose them.

When we entered Buck's shop, no one was at the counter. Benji placed the computer on the counter and rang the small bell that sat next to a sign that said *Ring me loud. Buck's deaf in one ear.*

When Buck didn't appear right away, Benji rang it again, this time longer and louder.

"No need to break the thing," Buck grumbled as he entered from the back. When he saw it was us, he grinned. "I should have expected as much from you. What are my two favorite people doing here on this lovely Sunday morning?"

I nodded to the box on the counter. "Flash says the computer is slow and randomly shutting down. He needs more memory, but he didn't tell me how much."

"Again? I just gave him more memory a few months ago. I better make sure he doesn't have a virus first. I know Flash is careful about that kind of thing, but it doesn't hurt to check." Buck opened the top of the box. "He knows how to do this stuff himself. Too busy?"

"Always and forever. When he isn't doing schoolwork, he's teaching the rest of the world how computer hacking is really done," I said with a laugh, but glanced at Benji to let him know it was his turn.

"Hey, Buck," Benji said, leaning against the counter. "I went to see Jake last night."

Buck stilled but quickly recovered and closed the flaps on the computer box. "Oh, yeah? I didn't know the sheriff was allowing anyone in. How's he doing?" He picked up the box and placed it on a counter that ran along the back wall.

"Good as could be expected, I suppose. Misses Angel and the kids."

Buck turned back to us and rested against the back counter. "I'd expect as much."

"He wants me to figure out who really started that fire —who framed him. Doesn't trust the sheriff to get it right. I was wondering if you'd help."

Buck rubbed the back of his neck, as if he was nervous. "I don't know, Benji. Getting involved in the sheriff's business doesn't seem like it would turn out well for anyone. Maybe we should leave this one to the professionals."

"The professionals," Benji muttered, shaking his head. "Come on, Buck. You know Sheriff Potts doesn't know this town like we do. She thinks one of us did it, and we need to prove her wrong."

That got Buck's attention.

"Is she nuts? We couldn't have anything to do with that construction site, and we certainly wouldn't set up our friend to take the fall. Especially not when that friend is Jake. Surely there has to be someone else."

Benji raised a shoulder. "There's not. Has she been by to talk to you about what happened that night?"

"Well, sure, she's visited half the town."

"What did you tell her?"

"That I skipped the town meeting to go out on a date, and I didn't get back until late. It can be verified by a dozen people." Buck puffed out his chest, as if he'd like to challenge anyone else to have a better alibi. He didn't mind being known around town as a womanizer—in fact, he relished it.

"None of her questions matter anyway," Benji said. "The fire started sometime in the middle of the night, when everyone was sleeping. No way to prove that people were in their bedrooms, so I don't know why she's bothering to go to the effort. What we need is clear, hard evidence that someone was outside their room, not inside."

Buck seemed a little queasy at the thought, and his smile seemed a little too wide as he agreed with Benji. "Don't know how you're going to manage that, but more power to you." He then turned to me. "Tell Flash I'll have this finished by end of day. You can pick it up first thing in the morning."

I took this to mean our time together was finished.

We only stayed a minute longer, and as we approached my car, I turned to Benji. "Well?"

"He didn't do it."

I raised a questioning eyebrow. "But you heard him, he doesn't want to get in the sheriff's way. There must be a reason for it."

"Yeah, there is. He hires a couple of local kids to help him out around the shop. Pays them cash each week so he doesn't have to claim it on his taxes. It's not completely honest, but I know how to read Buck. He's not our guy. Besides, more development in town means more dating opportunities for Buck. He won't sell his shop to the developers, but he doesn't mind benefiting if other people do."

I wasn't sure I agreed with Benji, but I was going to have to trust him on this one.

"Okay. We'll cross him off the list. Next stop is Cal's. What is our excuse going to be this time?"

Benji was looking at something down the street, and when I followed his gaze, I saw that Cal was standing on the sidewalk, his phone to his ear. And he was looking directly at us.

I glanced into Buck's shop through the front window. He was also on the phone.

We were going to need a good excuse for this one.

19

B enji threw on a smile and walked to where Cal was eyeing us with suspicion. "Cal, we were just on our way to see you."

The big man nodded slowly. "Yes, so I heard. From the way I hear it, you are looking into Jake's arrest and looking for recruits."

"We are. You know just as well as I do that Jake didn't do what he's being accused of, and his family doesn't deserve this. Angel is a wreck, and when I talked to her this morning, she said the twins are coming home tomorrow. It was her decision—she misses them and needs some sense of normalcy in her life, but it's not going to be the same if Jake isn't there with her to welcome them home."

Cal glanced up the street and back down, and then motioned for us to follow him into the bike shop. Once the door closed, he turned on us. "I know why you're really here."

I tried to act like I had no idea what he was talking about, but it was no use. I was as see-through as the bike shop's front window.

He nodded to me. "Yeah, that's what I thought. You think I framed Jake. Thought I would take matters into my own hands and then panicked when someone saw me in that bright pink hat." He frowned and glanced at Benji. "What kind of idiot wears a hat like that when burning down a building? I'm not the brightest guy out there, but I'm not that stupid."

"Where were you that night?" Benji asked, no longer bothering to hide our true intentions.

Cal frowned. "After the town meeting, I went home. You saw what a circus it was. The only thing I wanted to do was go to bed and pretend that none of this is happening. Pretend that our town isn't being torn apart. And pretend that if I just put my head in the sand, I can go on selling bikes like I've been doing for the past decade, without anyone bothering me." He released a heavy sigh. "I just needed to pretend, man."

"You went home right after the meeting?" I asked, perplexed.

"That's right." Cal met my gaze and held it, daring me to call him a liar.

Thankfully, Benji caught on. "We saw the light in your shop turn on and off as we were walking home that evening. I even checked the front door to make sure it was locked and that no one had broken in."

A flicker of panic crossed Cal's face, but it was gone just as quickly. It had been enough, though. I'd caught him in his lie.

"Like I said—"

The usually calm Benji cut him off. "Cal, you are one of the best people I know. Don't you dare lie to us and tell us you weren't here."

Cal opened his mouth to refute it but then wisely closed it again. And he stayed silent.

"You already admitted to trying to scare Don," I said, my voice quiet. "Maybe you can tell us what happened with the Parkside shops. We know you all decided to work together to get him to leave you alone. Was there any talk about burning down the construction site?"

Cal was already shaking his head. "No, nothing like that. Everything we discussed was harmless stuff. Jake said he was planning on hiking up his prices to exorbitant amounts, only for the developers, of course. Don's company was using other vendors for lumber and that kind of thing, but if Don forgot so much as a screwdriver, he'd be paying ten times what it cost somewhere else."

It made sense and was a relief that more drastic measures hadn't been considered.

"Then what were you doing here at your shop that night?" I asked. "Please. We're just trying to make sense of it all, and you do want to help Jake, don't you? Because for as long as you have all been friends, it seems you're more worried about yourself than what might become of him and his family. Frankly, you all are. Benji's the only one sticking his neck out, willing to ask the hard questions."

"Maybe it's because all the answers will point back to him," Cal snapped. "He's trying to create his own narrative."

Benji and I stared in dismay.

"What are you talking about?" Benji asked once he'd gotten over his shock at being accused of having something do with Don's death. "You think I'm involved? I'm a handyman. I have no motive. Yeah, I don't love the idea of our town changing, but neither do most people."

"So, it didn't bother you that a construction company was moving into Amor, permanently. And they wouldn't just handle new construction. They would handle comprehensive repair issues, both commercial and residential. There would be experts in electrical, plumbing, and everything in between. No need for a jack-of-all-trades when you can have the expert you need for your specific issue. At competitive rates, no less."

I looked to Benji. "You knew about this?"

No wonder he had been against the developers. No one was safe from their expansion—even our local handyman.

"Like I said, this isn't about me," Benji told Cal. "You know me better than that. Now, please answer the question. Why were you in your shop the night of the fire?"

"Because I am considering selling out, okay?" Cal half-yelled. He closed his eyes and pulled in a long breath, calming himself. "Not to Don. There's a new guy in town. He's been here a couple of times, all friendly with the mayor. I was here, in the dark, because I was looking at the contract he drew up. I didn't dare let anyone see, for obvious reasons. It turns out that the contract isn't half bad. I'd actually come out on top. You know what people would do if they found out, though, right? That's why I was huddled in the back of my bike shop reading a ridiculously long contract by only the light of my computer." He shook his head. "Of course, it might not even be an option at this point, with all the developers pulling out."

Cal selling to the developers. That wasn't what I had been expecting. And I would say that absolutely took him off our suspect list.

Of course, in the process, he'd demanded we add Benji to the list.

Not that I was considering that as a serious possibility.

Still, that didn't stop the sheriff's words from ringing in my ears. She had asked if Benji was any less likely than Cal or Lou to have started that fire. And if Benji was required to ask the hard questions of his closest friends, shouldn't I be expected to do the same?

Now that Benji had motive, I no longer knew the answer to that question.

Yes, I did.

With or without the hard questions, Benji was not a murderer.

"I CAN'T BELIEVE Cal would sell to the developers," Benji muttered as we left the shop. "If there was one person I thought we could count on to keep the developers at bay, it was him."

I didn't point out that that had been the exact reason Cal had been on our suspect list.

"He's doing what's best for his shop," I said. "It sounds like he can move to a better location and have money left over. I'd think you'd be happier for him. It also means he's no longer under suspicion."

Benji nodded, but his whole body drooped as we walked back to my car. Even after all the Sunday dinners when my mom and Benji would discuss local politics, and all the talk about how allowing outside developers would ruin the local New Mexican flavor that was so important to our identity, I hadn't realized how strongly Benji felt about it until this moment.

I should have listened more, but I usually tuned the two of them out because I'd rather stay silent than get mixed up in the discussion. It was the same reason I avoided town meetings. I had enough drama in my life; why invite more in?

"I'm sorry," I said, slipping my hand into his. "I know this is disappointing for you."

Benji rubbed a hand over his forehead. "Those guys at the

Parkside shops promised they would stand together. They all did things to scare Don Mendes into leaving, vowing to have each other's backs. That's not the kind of thing you do if you're planning on turning around and selling out to a different developer. I don't understand. Why would he do that?"

"Because in the end, people may say they are against the developers for the sanctity of the town, but in actuality, it's because they're scared," I said, releasing Benji's hand and moving to the driver's side door. "They are scared of how development will affect them personally. On an individual level. And selling to a decent developer who Mayor Freedman vouches for means that Cal doesn't have to live in fear anymore. He's taken control of his shop's future, and in a way that's beneficial for him."

"He's still living in fear," Benji said. "If people find out what he's about to do, his shop may be the next thing to burn."

I stood in the street, car door partially open, gaping at my boyfriend. "Careful what you say out here. That almost sounded like a threat."

Benji's lips dipped into a sad frown, and he shook his head. "Not a threat. It's just...people haven't been acting like themselves. Like you said, they are in self-preservation mode. They're scared. And they are turning against their neighbors."

My lips pressed into a firm line. "So, we keep Cal's secret, and we find the person who murdered Don. People need to feel comfortable voicing their opinions without fear of retaliation."

Benji gave a little nod but remained quiet.

"You don't still think Jake did it, do you?" I asked, concerned. I slipped into the driver's seat and shut my door.

Benji followed suit and then blew out a hard breath. "Honestly, I don't know what to think. And running around town accusing my friends of murder and arson and betrayal... I'd almost rather that Jake did it. At least then he'd have brought everything upon himself."

I spun toward Benji. "I can't believe you'd say that. Those twins need their dad. And we're going to give him to them. Do you understand me?"

Benji folded his arms across his chest and stared out the window. "Yes, ma'am."

The way he said it, it made me feel like I was a school-teacher and he was in trouble. We were supposed to be a team, working together. Not...whatever this was. But Benji had given up hope, and I didn't know where that left me.

I started the ignition. "My mom doesn't think Carlos did it," I said. "She talked with him last night. He's passion-ate, but he seems more concerned about Jake and Angel than anything else."

"So, you're saying you want to go investigate the next name on the list—Lou, our local firefighter and the man who found the body," Benji said, his gaze never straying from his window. His tone was emotionless. He'd checked out.

"Yes. But I'm dropping you off at home first. You're in no condition to come with me."

That got his attention.

He turned back to me, his gaze intense. "So you can go interrogate a potential murderer on your own? I don't think so. I may not be happy about the situation, but that doesn't mean I'm willing to put your life at risk."

At least he was finally accepting the fact that one of his friends may have done the unthinkable.

Of course, turning them over to the sheriff was another thing entirely.

20

It was Sunday, so Lou wouldn't be at the fire station. Not that we didn't have fires or gas leaks or car accidents on Sundays in Amor, but considering he was the only certified firefighter the town had, the volunteer firefighters took over on weekends. Which was ironically the two days that a fire was more likely to occur.

Benji glanced at his phone. "We have an hour until Lou leaves for church. Think that gives us enough time?"

"More than enough. We'll be lucky if we make it past the thirty-second mark." I took Benji's hand. I needed the extra reassurance. "Think Buck and Cal have called to let him know we've been by to visit?"

"Probably." Benji threw on a wide smile, though it was obviously forced. "So, this should be fun."

I pulled up in front of Lou's house, which sat just

around the corner from the fire station. Even though he took weekends off, he liked to stay in the loop.

Before we'd fully exited the car, Lou's front door swung open, and he was standing on his porch. As I stepped out and shut my door, I glanced at Benji, grimacing. "How do you want to do this?" I asked, my voice low.

Benji hadn't had the chance to answer when Lou strode up and wrapped Benji in a tight hug. "So glad you're here."

Not what I had been expecting.

Benji tentatively patted Lou on the back, then wriggled out of his grasp. "That's the best greeting we've received all day."

"Of course it is," Lou said, stepping back. "I always give the best hugs."

"Yeah, I know. It's just, not everyone has been pleased to see us. I'm sure Buck called you."

Lou motioned for us to follow him. "Cal, actually. Apparently, you two have taken on the role of vigilantes. You're looking to clear Jake's name. It's about time someone did something. I like Danielle Potts, and she's good at her job, but in this case, the evidence is wrong."

"How do you mean?" I asked as we followed Lou inside.

Lou led us to the dining room table where he already had food laid out. Sopapillas and honey sat next to small plates and a large pitcher of ice water. I silently thanked Cal for giving Lou a heads up, because this was probably the most delicious thing I was going to eat all week. Never underestimate the power of fried bread to defuse a situation.

"This looks amazing, Lou," I said, sitting down. "Did you make these?"

A grin spread across Lou's face, and he puffed out his chest a little. "Yup. Just this morning, so they're fresh."

"Thanks, Lou," Benji said. "You always were the best cook out of all of us." He paused as he took a plate and placed a sopapilla on it, then drizzled honey on top. "Why's the evidence wrong?"

Lou settled into a chair at the head of the table and leaned back, resting his hands on his stomach. "I don't care about eyewitnesses. They're unreliable. What I do know, and I've told the sheriff this, is that Don Mendes didn't die in that fire. Our arsonist is not our murderer."

"Right," I said, honey dripping down my chin. I grabbed a napkin to catch the honey, but then the paper stuck to my chin. Having grown up in New Mexico, I should have been better at eating these things. "Danielle told me that Don was attacked from behind, before the fire. But that doesn't mean the murderer and the arsonist aren't the same person. It makes sense that they'd start the fire to try to hide the evidence."

Lou nodded slowly. "Maddie, you're a psychologist. Tell me something. You have a person who kills someone by hitting them across the back of the head. Blunt force trauma. And then arranges for it to look like the victim had been sleeping before they sneak off. Let's say they sneak back to burn down the construction site. What is their fuel source?"

"I don't know much about arson," I said, wondering why Lou was asking me this. He clearly knew the correct answer. "Probably something that could make it look like an accident. Maybe there was some fuel already at the construction site that he was able to use."

Lou touched his nose, indicating I was right on the money. "Exactly. But that's not what our arsonist used."

"O-kay. I'll bite. How did the arsonist start the fire?"

"Pinecones," Lou said, reaching forward for a plate and a sopapilla.

Benji crinkled his nose as he passed Lou the honey. "Are you sure pinecones hadn't been blown onto the construction site by the wind or something?"

Lou nodded toward the front window. "Do you see any pine trees out there among the cactuses?" He gave a quick shake of his head. "No, the arsonist would have had to go to the mountains to get these particular ones. They're too big to be from someone's yard. I'd say they'd have to go at least an hour northeast from here."

That was very specific.

"Why pinecones?" I asked.

Lou ripped a chunk out of his sopapilla, sending honey all over his face. I was glad to know that there was no good way to eat these things. "They make excellent tinder, especially if they were dipped in wax." He grabbed at the stack of napkins. "The wax makes the pinecones burn longer and the fire start faster."

Pinecones. I'd have to remember that for the next time I went camping.

"You're saying," I said slowly, "that the type of person to take a bat or two by four to someone's head wouldn't be the type to have waxed pinecones sitting around."

Lou nodded, popping the rest of his sopapilla into his mouth, and then spoke around the food. "I could be wrong, of course. Maybe our killer is an outdoorsman. But more times than not, waxed pinecones are given as gifts and used to add decor to a home until they are needed. They'd likely be used in a residential fireplace. An outdoorsman doesn't bother dipping pinecones in wax. He finds his fuel source on the ground where he intends to camp."

"You're saying that the killer and the arsonist are two different people." I looked to Benji, realizing we'd made a mistake. "Is our arsonist a woman?"

Lou held up a finger. "Or a man who loves his crafts."

It could be. But I didn't think so. This entire time, I hadn't considered we could be looking for two different people, and it had certainly never crossed my mind that one of them could be a woman. With that shift in thinking, some of the pieces to this puzzle started clicking into place.

Unfortunately, I thought I knew who the arsonist was. And when I told Danielle Potts, she wasn't going to take me seriously. There was no way she'd make an arrest without either a confession or concrete evidence.

I needed to wait until I'd gathered everything.

Which meant I couldn't let on that Lou's revelation had meant anything to me.

"Huh," I said, attempting my most thoughtful expression. "That's something we'll need to keep in mind as we're talking with people. Thanks, Lou."

He nodded and scooted his chair back. I took that to mean our time together was over. Time for him to get ready for church. "No problem. Happy to help. Anything for Jake and Angel." He looked to Benji. "If there is anything I can do, please let me know. They're good people and don't deserve this."

Benji mirrored Lou, scooting his chair back, and I did the same.

"No, they don't," Benji agreed. He hesitated. "Lou, do you know what the murder weapon was?"

Lou shook his head. "Unfortunately, no. Either it burned in the fire or the killer took it with him...or her."

"I figured as much," Benji said. "Did Sheriff Potts have any theories about whether it was premeditated or a crime of passion?"

"No idea. Though I will say that Don Mendes didn't have to be lured anywhere, because he had his whole bed made up on that concrete slab. Had his suitcase too. Seemed like he was afraid to return to his hotel room and decided to set up camp for the night. Maybe someone followed him there."

"Why not just leave town, then, if he was so afraid?" I mused.

"Might have something to do with not having a way out," Benji said, tossing me a glance. "With no public transportation, he would have had to call the shuttle service, and they don't operate late. He probably figured he could hightail it out of here first thing in the morning. Maybe after his meeting with you."

I didn't have time for maybes.

Jake had less than twenty-four hours, and then none of it would matter.

21

By the time Benji and I returned home, my mind was buzzing, but my body was exhausted. As soon as I entered the house, I slipped off my shoes and collapsed onto the couch.

"What a day," I said, closing my eyes and nestling into the cushions. "And it's only noon."

Benji sat down at the other end of the couch and placed my feet on his lap. When he began massaging them, a small groan escaped my lips. This was a man who knew how to treat me well.

So, why did I freak out every time he brought up our future together? Why couldn't I just enjoy the small moments that led to the bigger moments that led to the happiest life I could imagine?

"Benji?" I said, my eyes still closed as he worked his thumbs near my heel.

"Hmmm?"

"You know I love you, right?" I opened one eye and saw he was smiling.

"Yes, I know."

I closed it again. "Good."

We were silent for another minute as he switched to my other foot.

"Maddie?"

"Hmmm?"

A pause.

"I know I promised I wouldn't bring it up again. But I can't help it. After we prove Jake is innocent, can we talk more about our future together? I'm trying to pretend it doesn't matter to me—that as long as I'm with you, in whatever capacity that is, it's fine by me. But the truth is, it's not. I love that we're dating, and I still can't believe you chose me. I get to spend every day with my best friend and the woman I love. But it's not the same thing as being married. You act like I'm already a part of your family, but I'm not. We still have our separate lives, and…it's different."

My eyes opened, and I pushed myself up onto my elbows. "Benji, I'm not going anywhere. We have time to figure this out. There's no hurry."

I tried to sound calm, but my heart was pounding against my ribs and my anxiety rising. It was all the pressure from my mom and the neighbors…and now Benji. Avoiding the discussion was no longer working, and it left me wondering if I was meant to ever be in another long-term committed relationship. Everything was great with Benji, as long as we stayed in the moment. But when we strayed too far, that was when my instincts told me to run.

I didn't want to—but it felt like it was a matter of survival. Like if I didn't create some distance, my heart, and my head, were going to implode.

Love shouldn't feel like that.

Benji pulled back, and I immediately missed his touch. "I know. I'm sorry. It's just...hard to wait sometimes. I've loved you since we were teenagers, and it nearly broke my heart when you left town. And now to have you back—it's something I never dared dream possible. But sometimes I feel like that dream is so close and yet still so far. Like I'm being kept at arm's length. Just in case."

Just in case.

As much as Benji's words stung, I understood what he was saying. Because that was exactly what I'd been doing.

"Benji..."

The sounds of people storming into the house broke my train of thought.

I swung my legs off Benji's lap just as Flash and Lilly burst into the front room. "What on earth is going on?"

"We found the murder weapon," Lilly said, out of breath. Her camera hung around her neck, looking heavy as it swung back and forth.

Flash nodded vigorously, but no sound escaped his moving lips.

I exchanged panicked looks with Benji. Whatever they'd found, it couldn't be good.

Lilly continued when her brother didn't. "I thought the burned-out construction site might make for some cool photographs and took my camera out there. When I was trying to get a different angle by climbing down into a nearby ditch, I found it lying at the bottom, like someone had panicked and tossed it the first place they could think of."

They both stared at us like they were awaiting some kind of reaction.

They got it.

"Are you kidding me?" Benji asked, leaping to his feet. "How did the sheriff overlook that? What was the murder weapon?"

"Bob's missing gavel," I muttered, realizing just how much I'd missed. "Last seen at the town meeting the night Don Mendes died."

Aw, crap.

Flash raised his eyebrows and nodded. "Yeah. Lilly called me as soon as she found it, and I raced out there to help her figure out what to do. There's still some blood on it."

"Where is it now?" I said, glancing at my phone. Twelve-thirty. Church services were just starting. It was non-denominational because there weren't enough people in town to support more than one church. That meant everyone would be in the same place for the next hour.

Lilly held up her camera bag. "I put it in here. It shouldn't have any of my fingerprints on it. I used my lens cleaning cloth to pick it up."

"Thanks." I took the bag from her. "I'll get you a new one."

I looked at the bag, not daring to open it. I didn't want to see the gavel, or the blood. And I certainly didn't want to think about what this meant. I had no choice, though. We were running out of time.

Benji's eyebrows scrunched in concern, and he glanced at me. "You figured it out, didn't you?"

I nodded. "On a scale of one to ten, how mad do you think God will be if the sheriff makes an arrest or two at the church? One is *He won't care at all and instead be grateful that justice is served*, and ten is *The ten plagues of Egypt will descend upon Amor and wipe out all the first born*."

"I'd say a four," Flash said, finding his voice. "He'll care a bit, but not as much as Pastor Franks. I've heard he gets a bit worked up during his sermons."

One of the many reasons I hadn't attended church since leaving for college. If I wanted to feel guilty about everything I was, or wasn't, doing, I had my neighbor Edna for that.

"Does Danielle attend church services?" I asked Benji while slipping on my shoes.

Unlike me, Benji was a regular churchgoer. Today had been an exception. He'd said he thought God would understand if he helped free an innocent man in lieu of church services.

"She attends in uniform and always stands at the back. She acts like she's just there to keep the peace, but there's only been three fights that have broken out in the past six months. I personally think she's there because she wants to be."

"That makes things easier," I said, slinging Lilly's camera bag over one shoulder.

"Can I come?" Flash asked. "Grandma would be happy to see me at church. It's been a while."

I held back a laugh because I knew exactly why he wanted to come, and it had nothing to do with religion. "You know I can't let you do that."

"But I'm practically an adult," he protested. "Give or take a year or two. Besides, if you don't let me go to church and it's your fault I don't get into heaven, God is not going to be happy with you."

Lilly smirked and shook her head. "Nice try, but when you live under Mom's roof, you have to play by her rules." She then turned to me. "I, on the other hand, am legally an adult and can make my own choices. And today that means attending church with you."

"I appreciate everything you've done," I said with a patient smile. "But you need to stay here with your brother and keep him out of trouble. Besides, you always said church was boring."

Benji released a long breath. "That shows how long it's

been since you've attended. A couple weeks ago, Pastor Franks was preaching about forgiveness, but Edna stood up in the middle of his sermon and said she'd never forgive Debbie for the haircut she was given. Apparently, Edna had told Debbie she wanted her to use her creativity to give Edna a new look, as long as Debbie didn't give her bangs. Debbie thought Edna said she wanted bangs, so of course Edna now has the best-looking bangs in town, but you can see where this is going. Long story short, someone being arrested for murder will not be the craziest thing that's happened in that church this month."

Well, alrighty then.

To the church it was.

I didn't love the idea of crashing Pastor Franks' sermon, but it was the only time everyone would be together before our deadline was up.

If the sheriff waited until after church and tried to arrest the culprits separately, our town's gossip train would ensure that the other would catch wind of what she was doing and they'd hightail it before she had the chance.

No, it had to be now.

22

The church in Amor wasn't big. It was likely half the size of what would be expected in the city, but I wouldn't know. This was the only church I'd ever attended. And every week, every pew was filled. It could be one of the reasons Sheriff Potts always stood in the back. Well, that and she had to be at the ready, just in case Edna came home with another unsatisfactory haircut.

"You sure you want to do this?" Benji whispered.

I gave a sharp nod. "I called Danielle, and it went straight to voicemail. Coming here is the only way we'll be able to speak with her in time."

His eyes lit up in understanding. "Oh, yes. I don't blame her for turning off her phone. If a phone goes off during the service, Pastor Franks confiscates it and doesn't give it back until that evening. He says it's to teach a lesson on how important it is to put our worldly possessions aside and keep our focus on the things that truly matter. He doesn't care if you're the sheriff."

That didn't exactly make me feel bad about missing church all these years.

"Once the service ends, we lose our window of opportunity," I said, taking a step forward.

Benji nervously looked to the front doors. "This is going to be the town meeting all over again. We go in with guns blazing, the place is going to empty out, and we'll be left empty-handed."

That was a very good point.

I stopped and turned back.

"So, what do you suggest?"

Benji gave me an apologetic smile. "It will be suspicious if you go in, considering you haven't stepped foot in this church since you were a teenager. Maybe you can wait out here while I get the sheriff's attention."

I didn't love the thought of being stuck outside, but Benji was right. It would raise too many eyebrows.

With a quick kiss, I wrapped my arms around his waist. "I'm not here for me—it's for Jake. You do what you need to do to make sure he doesn't spend another night in jail."

He smiled down on me, kissed my forehead, then stepped back. "In that case, wish me luck." And then he slipped through the front doors, leaving me pacing anxiously as I awaited his and the sheriff's return.

It couldn't have been more than five minutes before

Benji returned, though Danielle reached me first, her forehead wrinkled with worry.

"Please tell me you don't expect me to arrest someone during our church service. People already don't know what to make of the fact that your family doesn't attend. This is only going to make things worse."

I hesitated. "You'll be arresting two people, actually. One for arson, and one for murder. Though I'm still unsure if the latter was premeditated. That will be for you to figure out."

Danielle shook her head. "Great. Thanks." She glanced toward the front doors, just as Benji had done several minutes earlier, as if there was something in there that made her nervous. "I don't think Jake burned down the construction site. You know I don't. But how certain are you that you've pegged the correct people? This isn't something I can afford to be wrong about. I have to either charge Jake or let him go. That means you only have one shot."

My heart thudded with anxiety. How sure was I? "Ninety-five percent," I said, thinking that was pretty good.

Danielle folded her arms across her chest. "Not good enough."

Oh. She wanted me super-duper sure. "And when I say ninety-five percent, I mean more like ninety-nine percent. I don't believe anyone should be one-hundred percent certain about anything."

I could tell Danielle was torn between wanting to find

someone—anyone other than Jake—guilty for these crimes and wanting to make sure she wasn't making a mistake. "I'm not going back in there until you give me names and probable cause. It's both Jake's life and my reputation on the line, and I'm not willing to put either at risk by going into this unprepared."

Couldn't argue with that.

"All right," I said, running my fingers through my hair. The whole thing sounded crazy in my head; I could only imagine how it would sound when I said it out loud. "Let's start with Don's murder."

WHILE I EXPLAINED, Danielle paced in front of the church, muttering to herself. Something about how she was about to be run out of town and it was all my fault. I didn't blame her. Arresting Jake hadn't exactly made her popular with the locals, but the alternative was about to make everything worse.

I cleared my throat and held up a finger. "Danielle, I'm sorry, I don't mean to rush you. But you only have twenty minutes before this place clears out and you lose your opportunity."

She glanced toward me, panic etched in her features. "This is ludicrous. You know that, right?"

"Yes, I do. And I'm sorry to put you in this position, but you once told me that you are bound to go where the evidence leads. Do you agree that this is where it has led?"

With a slow nod, she said, "I do. It doesn't mean I have to like it, though." She glanced over her shoulder, no doubt looking for her deputy. As much as she appreciated my and Benji's help, she had been absolutely right to call her deputy for back-up. This one was brand new, though, having arrived just a month earlier, and she hadn't had to rely on him for something like this before. Hopefully he was as good as Danielle said he was.

It seemed she went through deputies like Flash went through pizza, but in all fairness, it was difficult to attract law enforcement who wanted to live someplace as quiet as Amor. At least, as quiet as it had been before the developers had shown up.

Her deputy, Michael, pulled up in the squad car, and with his arrival, I could see Danielle's whole body loosen, the stress leaving her. After briefing him quickly on the situation, she squared her shoulders and stepped toward the church.

The plan was that she'd confront both suspects with her deputy blocking the exit. Yes, it was a fire hazard to have only one exit, especially with the amount of candle lighting that went on in there, but no one had cared enough to do anything about it.

Besides, if anything went wrong and a fire broke out, they had Lou to take care of it.

Benji and I entered first. Of course, every head turned as the door squeaked, everyone wondering who the late-comers were. If Pastor Franks was surprised to see me inside his church, he didn't let on, not missing a beat as he preached patience and long-suffering.

That didn't stop a hundred other looks of surprise from following us as we struggled to find a seat. Unable to find anything that wouldn't involve climbing over a dozen laps, we gave up and stood at the back.

Edna turned in her seat and whisper-yelled, "It's about time. I knew if I kept asking, it would eventually wear you down."

If she only knew the real reason I was here.

I gave her a tight smile and pointed at the pastor, like I wanted to hear what he had to say.

Danielle entered the church next. She glanced around the room, her gaze scanning for the two people who were going to need a lot of patience and long-suffering where they would be going.

It wasn't until Michael took his place in front of the back doors that people started really taking notice. The whispers began to escalate, and more heads turned.

To Pastor Franks' credit, he managed to ignore it far longer than I would have been able to. Eventually it was too much for even him, and he ended early, as if that had been the plan all along.

Before he could say a final prayer, however, Danielle stepped forward.

"I'm so sorry to have to do this, Pastor," she said, "but there is a small matter that needs to be addressed before everyone adjourns for the day. It won't take more than a minute."

Murmurs broke out, and the pastor looked like he was about to protest, but Danielle quickly continued, not giving him the chance.

"This camera bag contains the murder weapon that killed Don Mendes," she said, lifting Lilly's bag high in the air. "Bob's gavel from the town meeting Thursday evening."

"Are you kidding me?" Bob shouted. "When my gavel went missing, I thought it was a jealous town council member, or maybe a punk kid playing a prank. But a murder weapon—well, that blood is never coming out. And now someone owes me a new gavel."

Edna yelled back at him, "Says the man whose gavel was the murder weapon. Maybe you only said it was missing because you knew what it had really been used for."

"You think I had something to do with this?" Bob released a humorless laugh. "This proves what I've been telling people for years. Edna's gone crazy."

Pastor Franks was no longer trying to stop the sheriff. Instead, he leaned forward with the rest of the congregation, not wanting to miss a word. You couldn't pay for this kind of drama.

Sheriff Potts continued, trying to be heard above the murmuring that had broken out. "This gavel has the fingerprints of the killer on it. And they are not Jake Pletcher's. He is innocent."

I hadn't seen Angel sitting in the third row until she let out a cry of disbelief. She buried her face in her hands, sobbing.

"Thank goodness," Carlos Herrera exclaimed, jumping to his feet. "This is a day to rejoice and give thanks to God."

And then he did something remarkably stupid. He ran for the door.

23

I'd had my suspicions that Carlos Herrera was likely the murderer, given his close proximity to the gavel at the end of the town meeting and his intense feelings toward Don Mendes and the rest of the developers. But I hadn't been the ninety-nine percent sure I had led Danielle to believe. It had seemed too obvious. This was a man who had never bothered to hide his disdain for Don Mendes, even after Don turned up dead.

What I had counted on was the killer panicking when he found out about the fingerprints. The sheriff had led everyone to believe that we knew whose fingerprints were on the gavel. In actuality, I had handed her the murder weapon only a few minutes before she'd entered the church. There had been no time for analysis.

I'd thought the murderer would panic, but even so, I didn't understand what Carlos thought was going to happen when he ran, considering both the sheriff and deputy were at the back of the room, literally standing in front of the door. All Michael had to do was open his arms and catch Carlos. Granted, Carlos was much faster and more agile than I'd expected, vaulting over church pews as he made his run for it.

But ultimately, he and Michael went crashing to the floor together, and when they stood back up, Carlos was already in handcuffs.

Angel was now on her feet, wiping at her tear-stained cheeks and glaring angrily in Carlos's direction. "After Jake was arrested, you came by to check on me and the kids. When I wouldn't allow anyone in, you left gifts," she said, her voice cracking. Her words rang through the church. "And all this time, it was to throw suspicion off the fact that you framed Jake. We've invited you over for dinner— treated you well. What did Jake do to deserve this kind of treatment?"

"I didn't betray him," Carlos said, desperate pleading in his tone. "It's true that I did kill Don, but I didn't mean to. And I certainly didn't start that fire or frame Jake. I would never do that."

"And yet you didn't come forward," Angel said, her sadness beginning to turn to anger. "You left presents because of the guilt you felt, but all the gifts in the world wouldn't make up for what you did."

"Why should I be punished for something that was an accident?" Carlos asked, squirming under the entire room's gaze. "Don Mendes wanted to purchase everyone else's shops but wouldn't give me the time of day. Said my store wasn't in a location he was interested in, and it wasn't worth what I thought it was. No one ever thinks I'm special enough or desirable enough. I'm tired of people ignoring me. So yes, I went to his hotel room when he wasn't there and searched for anything that could give me leverage over him. There was nothing there, and I had no choice but to follow him the night of the town meeting. I just wanted to have a little chat. Help him see what a terrible mistake he was making. I followed him all the way from the hotel to that blasted construction site. But you know what he did? He laughed at me. And something inside me snapped. I decided that would be the last time anyone ever laughed at me again."

The room was silent. This was a man who had been in direct defiance against the real estate developers, and yet here he was admitting that he'd begged Don Mendes to purchase his shop, and then killed Don when he refused.

"Why?" Bob said, asking what everyone was thinking. "Why did you so desperately need him to purchase your shop? Yours is the only outdoor recreation store in town, and I've seen your quarterly taxes at Town Hall. I know you do good business."

"Not good enough," Carlos said. "Not enough to cover my debts. If Don had purchased my store, I could have left this town and started a new life. A place where no one knew me—where no one looked at me with pity and only included me when they felt bad for me." He threw a glance toward Angel. "Like the Pletchers."

Angel's eyes narrowed.

"Don't get me wrong," Carlos continued. "I do feel bad about you and Jake getting pulled into this mess, and I appreciate everything you've done for me over the years, but ultimately, it was better that it was him than me. It was a matter of self-preservation. You understand that, don't you?"

Good thing Angel didn't have her gun at that moment. Her nostrils flared with rage, and Cal had to keep her from leaping over the pew at Carlos.

"You feel bad, sure," she spat. "So bad that you used one of Jake's lighters to torch the construction site after you killed Don. Of course, you were too stupid to torch the murder weapon while you were at it."

I lifted a finger and stepped forward, feeling like this had gone on long enough. I threw a glance at Danielle, and she gave a small nod. "Carlos is telling the truth," I said. "He didn't start the fire. Even though he absolutely intended on threatening Don, and scaring him a bit, I don't believe he intended on killing him. It seems reasonable that in that situation, he'd torch the place and get out of there, but he didn't. Instead, he ran, much like today. As he did so, he threw the gavel into a nearby ditch. I don't think there was any reasoning behind the action, other than what he cares about most—survival." I paused and pulled in a deep breath. Before entering the church, I had told

Danielle I would handle this part. Now I had no idea what I'd been thinking.

"Well, who started the fire, then?" Angel asked impatiently.

My gaze landed on Edna. "Someone who loves this town very much and had no idea that a few hours earlier, Don Mendes had been murdered in that very spot."

Edna's face paled. "I—but—how could you possibly know that?"

"You never meant to frame Jake," I said, my voice kind. Edna might have caused me all sorts of grief as my neighbor over the years, but she wasn't mean-spirited, and I hated that I had to do this. But just before coming in here, I'd realized no one would have taken Danielle seriously if she'd accused my elderly neighbor of arson. A woman who sold ceramic frogs at the Saturday market and was equivalent to the town's nosy grandmother.

"It was you who wore the pink walkathon hat because that's what you do," I continued. "You walk. Everywhere. Constantly. And driving a couple of hours so you could support Jake in memory of his sister who died of cancer—that didn't seem like too much to ask."

Edna bent her head. "I meant to tell someone. And I think I would have, eventually. But you have to understand, I was scared. Up until five minutes ago, I thought I'd accidentally killed someone." She looked back up at me. "How was someone like me going to survive in prison? I've watched movies. I know how it works in there. It's all about how tough you are, and who you know. No one would want me in their prison gang for obvious reasons, so I'd be left with no protection."

I tried not to smile, even though Edna was being completely adorable in that moment. "You do know that you still need to stand trial for what you've done."

Edna waved a hand through the air. "Yes, I'm well aware. But they don't put arsonists in the same place as murderers. I figure I can charm my way into a lighter sentence."

If the warden was looking for someone to tattle on the other inmates, she might be right about that. It was very possible her keen observation and gossip skills could be her saving grace in this situation.

"Just one more thing," Edna said as she stood, preparing to go with the sheriff. "How did you know it was me wearing that hat? I'd only grabbed it because it was the first one I saw, but I wasn't the only one in town with the same pink hat."

I smiled. "No, but no one else in town would make a fire starter out of pinecones dipped in wax. You are the crafty one of Amor, certainly more so than Jake and his bachelor friends. When I first saw the spatters on your driveway, I thought it was paint. It wasn't until I was told about the fire starter that I realized it was wax."

Edna snapped her fingers. "Oh, darn. Well, just know that I had intended on making those fire starters for Christmas presents. They are quite festive when displayed and then look marvelous in the fireplace. They burn real good too, as you know." She held up a finger, like she'd just thought of something. "There are still a couple dozen of them sitting on my kitchen counter. Feel free to give them out if I'm not home in time."

That was positive thinking, considering Christmas was only three months away.

"I'd be happy to do that for you."

I turned away, unable to bear watching the sheriff lead Edna out. At least Danielle didn't use the handcuffs. I wasn't usually concerned that arsonists be allowed a little dignity when being arrested, but this was different.

This was Edna.

Of course, Carlos Herrera was another matter. He kicked and screamed the entire way, and it didn't bother me one bit.

At least he'd have a change of scenery like he'd wanted.

I slipped my hand into Benji's and, with a final glance at Pastor Franks, who had sat down and was looking a little worse for wear, we stepped back out into the sun.

"How was your first time back in church?" Benji teased. "Think you'll become a regular?"

I squeezed his hand. "If the arrest rate in the congregation is anything to go by, I might sit this one out a little longer."

Benji laughed, but his smile quickly faded. "I know I shouldn't feel bad for Carlos—but I kinda do. Maybe if I had been kinder to him over the years, and included him more, he wouldn't have felt the need to do something so drastic. He would have had a friend to hear about his struggles with debt—a support system."

I stopped mid-step and turned Benji toward me. "You can't blame yourself for what he's done. When something like this happens, people tend to look back on themselves and wonder how they could have prevented the tragedy. But we can't be a friend and a confidant to every person we meet, and sometimes a smile and a hello is the best we can do."

Benji nodded and pulled me into a tight hug. I could hear his heart beating in his chest, and it immediately comforted me. Because I'd been feeling guilty too. It didn't make any sense, but I felt like I was the reason an old lady was going to prison. Even though, like the sheriff, I had only gone where the evidence had led me.

My breath stalled, and I pulled back.

By that line of logic, if I really intended to go where the evidence led me, I'd made some serious blunders in the past few weeks.

I just hoped it wasn't too late to fix them.

B enji and I walked through downtown Amor, my hand in his, and I breathed in a lungful of the crisp fall air. I glanced at Benji, so grateful for this moment. Not speaking. Just enjoying each other's company.

We turned down the small path by Cal's bike shop, and I looked through the window. Buck was inside, leaning on the counter and laughing hysterically at something Cal had said. When Cal had told people he was selling to a new developer, Stephen McAllister, no one had been surprised. They'd all been contacted as well and were impressed with what was being offered.

The result was that these Parkside shops weren't going to be here much longer, but that didn't mean they were disappearing. If anything, they were going to be bigger and brighter than before, just in a different location.

We rounded the corner, and our expansive park was

suddenly in front of us, one of the few places you could find large, mature trees in Amor. Jake, Angel, and the twins were playing chase together at the other end. I couldn't believe that just a week earlier, Angel had pulled a gun on me, Jake had been in jail, and their entire future had hung in the balance.

No more.

Justice had been served, although we all fully expected Edna to show back up here any day. She would be released on bail and then manage to sweet-talk the jury with her elderly charms. That was mostly because they didn't have to live next to her. If they had been her neighbor for the past few years, they might not be so accommodating.

Benji leaned down and kissed me on the forehead, lingering, before he straightened.

"Did you just smell me?" I asked, looking up at him and laughing.

He raised a shoulder and smiled. "I like your new shampoo. It smells like peaches."

I was both flattered and worried that meant he was going to be randomly smelling me from there on out. It wasn't that I minded...much...but it did make me feel a bit self-conscious. What if I didn't smell like peaches the next day? What if I had been in a hurry and forgotten to put on deodorant?

"Maybe I should buy you your own shampoo. That way you can smell it anytime you want."

He laughed and pulled me into a side hug. "That's why

I have you. Forever and always." As soon as the words left his lips, I felt him tense. "Sorry, I know that kind of talk makes you uncomfortable. What I meant to say is—"

Seeing how quickly Benji went from easygoing to feeling he had to apologize for flirting with me, it made me sad. I loved Benji, and I didn't want him feeling like he needed to walk on eggshells whenever we were together, always afraid he'd say the wrong thing because I'd been having anxiety issues around our relationship.

That needed to end now.

Our love needed to be unconditional. Because I did want to be with him forever and always. There would never be anyone else.

"Benji, stop," I said, pulling away, though my hand lingered in his.

"I said I'm sorry—"

"And you shouldn't have to," I interrupted. "You deserve better than that."

He was now looking nervous, and I realized he thought I was about to break up with him. I needed to put a stop to those thoughts as quickly as possible.

So, I dropped to one knee.

Now he was looking a completely different type of nervous. "What are you—"

My anxiety matched his, but now that I was down on the ground, there was only one thing to do about it.

"Benjamin Matkin, I have been unfair to both you and myself. All evidence points to the fact that I love you. And will, forever and always. Just like you've been by my side through rain and sunshine, you deserve someone who will give you the same." I paused and pulled in a long breath. "Benji, will you marry me?"

I thought he was going to fall over, his mouth hanging open, staring at me, and I didn't blame him. I couldn't believe I'd just done that. My heart was racing, and I felt like I was going to throw up. I was just as nervous that he was going to accept my offer as I was that he'd reject it.

"I know this is sudden," I said, beginning to stand, feeling silly down on one knee, as Benji struggled to find words. "And I don't have a ring..."

But then I heard from the distance, "Maddison Swallows, you stay down there until that boy gives you an answer."

My mom.

Why was she here? I spun around and discovered her sitting on a nearby park bench, Trish and both kids sitting with her.

They were all here.

And Lilly was filming the event.

"How did you know?" I asked.

My mom winked at me. "A mother always knows. That, and Lilly said you were acting more anxious than usual. We thought something like this might be happening and didn't want to miss out."

I sincerely hoped Benji said yes, or this could be a very

embarrassing moment that was now preserved on video for years to come.

When I looked back to him, he still stood there, silent, but he had moisture in his eyes. I couldn't tell if that was a good thing or a bad thing. And then he dropped to his knees so that he was looking into my eyes.

"Are you sure?" he asked, taking both of my hands in his. "If you felt pressured in any way to do this, please know that wasn't my intention. I can wait as long as you need."

I stopped his words with a kiss.

"I want this," I said breathlessly against his lips. "And I don't want to wait any longer. When I look back, I realize we've waited our entire lives for this."

A grin erupted over Benji's face, and he pressed his lips hard against mine. "Then yes. Of course I'll marry you."

"It's about time," my mom yelled, then she and the rest of the family whooped and hollered and ran over to us, tackling us to the ground.

I laughed, a thrill of excitement making me smile so wide, my cheeks hurt.

It was unreal. I, Maddie Swallows, was getting married. Not only that, but I was marrying the one man who made me feel like I deserved every good thing in the world, even when I was less than perfect. The man who made me laugh and who was by my side when I cried. The man who made me want to be better, and to make the world better.

The man who was always there for my kids, even though they weren't his.

I was marrying my best friend.

Now, how to get out from under this dogpile so I could share my announcement with the rest of the world.

EPILOGUE

8 months later

Trish's cat, Ava, ran between my legs as I flipped the waffle maker, another perfectly crisp Belgium waffle landing on my plate. I'd bought myself the waffle maker at the same time I'd replaced my mom's.

"Who wants more?" I called out.

Benji and the kids groaned in response as Trish jumped up from the table and carried her plate to the sink.

"I don't think I'll ever be able to eat another waffle again," Flash said, pushing his empty plate towards Lilly. She pushed it back.

I had never seen Flash turn down food. "You okay?" I

asked, concerned. "I could call Dr. Harris and see if he can stop by."

My mom walked into the room, but when she saw me with the waffle, she made a quick U-turn.

I scrunched my nose and placed a hand on my hip. "Okay, what's going on with you guys? You're all acting weird."

Trish stepped around me to place her plate in the dishwasher. She glanced at me, and I could see there was something she wanted to tell me, but she was too scared to say it.

I put my food down and waved a hand through the air. "Out with it."

She hesitated. "Don't be mad. We appreciate everything you've been doing around here. But the past three weeks have been an endless train of waffles and smiley face pancakes and spaghetti and pizza and cookies and decorative fruit art, not to mention the organizing of the closets, and our bedrooms, and the kitchen..."

"I still haven't been able to figure out where the steak knives are," Benji added. As soon as the words left his mouth, his lips clamped shut, like he shouldn't have brought attention to himself.

My lips dipped in confusion. "You guys are mad that I've been ultra-productive and been feeding you all sorts of amazing food?"

"Not mad," my mom said, daring to poke her head

around the corner. "Overwhelmed. You're nervous about the upcoming wedding, and we get that. But the anxiety has been fueling your crazy side. There's no room left in the refrigerator because of all the leftovers, and yet you continue to cook five times more than any of us can eat. And considering Flash's appetite, that's saying something. That wouldn't be so bad if we could find where anything was, but every time we figure it out, you've reorganized again and it's in a different location."

I was tempted to be offended, but the psychologist side of me forced me to take a step back and analyze if what they were saying was valid.

It didn't take much self-reflection to realize they weren't exaggerating. It was that bad.

I looked down at the waffle on my plate. It looked amazing, but I hadn't stopped long enough to realize I was so full, I had made myself feel sick.

"The wedding is only three months away, but we've done everything there is to do," I said. "The venue, food, flowers, cake, dress, photographer, invitations... It's all done. And now I have all this time, and all I can do is wait and make myself crazy. Keeping myself busy is the only way I know how to stay sane. But it seems even that wasn't enough."

My mom finally summoned the courage to fully enter the kitchen, and she gave me an understanding smile. "Why don't you close the therapy office for a week and go on a road trip with Benji and the kids? It will help get your mind off things, and because Flash just graduated, and Lilly accepted that job in California, this could be the perfect opportunity for you all to head out and do one last thing as a family."

If my mom was trying to help me feel better, she'd failed. Just the thought of my kids leaving me sent me into hives. What if Lilly didn't like her co-workers? What if she had a difficult time navigating such a big city? What if Flash got arrested because he'd walked such a fine line with his hacking skills over the years, he had accidentally crossed that line without even realizing it?

I squeezed my eyes shut. When I reopened them, the rest of my family was watching with concern.

My mom was right. I needed to get out of town. Get my mind off things. And enjoy this time with my family.

"All right. A road trip it is," I said. "What do you think of Carlsbad Caverns? I've never been and hear it's incredible. There are over a hundred caves, with some of them so large and beautiful, they're like an underground cathedral."

I paused, and my kids stared at me, their expressions blank.

"And," I continued, "there are places so deep and dark that when they turn the lights off, you can't see your hand in front of your face. The bats love it. And this time of year, you will see plenty of them."

My kids cheered.

"I get to choose the road trip music, right?" Lilly asked.

"And I get to choose the snacks," Flash added.

I motioned toward the fridge. "What do you mean? We have all the snacks we need. A hundred waffles, four pizzas, and a carved-out watermelon filled with fruit in the shape of ladybugs."

Benji and the kids' mouths opened like they wanted to protest but couldn't find the words.

I laughed. "Just kidding. I'm never eating another waffle again. Or at least not for a very long time."

Relief passed over their features, and Benji scooted back his chair. "I'll let Jake know we'll be heading out of town. I'm sure he can cover any repairs that pop up while we're gone." He walked over and kissed me, sending tingles down to my toes, reminding me that I wasn't anxious about marrying Benji. I was a wreck because it couldn't happen soon enough.

"This will be just what we need," I said. "As long as we don't discover any bodies at the bottom of these caverns. They check for those kinds of things, right?"

"Probably, but I doubt they have the kind of bad luck you do," my mom said, pulling out a bag of leftover waffles and throwing it in the trash. She glanced at me. "With your luck, you'll find an entire lost civilization down there, all slaughtered with no one knowing who did it or why."

"Good thing I'm not an archeologist, then," I said, smiling.

She harrumphed. "They'll find a way to drag you into things. They always do."

The End

CHOOSE YOUR OWN ADVENTURE: MYSTERY OR ROMANCE

MADDIE SWALLOWS MYSTERIES

Dead Before Dinner

Dead Upon Arrival

Dead Before I Do

Dead Among Stars

Dead by Design

Dead in the Dark

BORROWING AMOR: New Mexican Romance

Borrowing Amor

Borrowing Love

Borrowing a Fiancé

Borrowing a Billionaire

Borrowing Kisses

Borrowing Second Chances

STARLIGHT RIDGE: Beach Romance

Diving into Love

Resisting Love

Starlight Love

Building on Love

Winning his Love

Returning to Love

Fearless Love

ABOUT THE AUTHOR

Kat Bellemore is the author of both the Borrowing Amor small town romance series and the Maddie Swallows cozy mystery series. Deciding to have New Mexico as the setting for these series was an easy choice, considering its amazing sunsets, blue skies and tasty green chile. That, and she currently lives there with her husband and two cute kids. They hope to one day add a dog to the family, but for now, the native animals of the desert will have to do. Though, Kat wouldn't mind ridding the world of scorpions and centipedes. They're just mean.

You can visit Kat at www.kat-bellemore.com.